# THE

# Washingtonienne

THE

# Washingtonienne

Jessica Cutler

HYPERION   New York

Library of Congress Cataloging-in-Publication Data

Cutler, Jessica.
  The Washingtonienne / by Jessica Cutler.
    p.   cm.
    ISBN: 1-4013-0200-9
    1. Capitol Hill (Washington, D.C.)—Fiction.   2. Internship
programs—Fiction.   3. Washington (D.C.)—Fiction.   I. Title.

PS3603.U85W37   2005
813'.6—dc22

2005040245

PAPERBACK ISBN: 1-4013-0847-3

Hyperion books are available for special promotions and
premiums. For details contact Michael Rentas, Assistant
Director, Inventory Operations, Hyperion, 77 West 66th Street,
11th floor, New York, New York 10023, or call 212-456-0133.

Designed by Lorelle Graffeo

FIRST U.S. PAPERBACK EDITION

10  9  8  7  6  5  4  3  2  1

*For Alethea*

# THE

# Washingtonienne

*Chapter 1*

J ust between us girls, Washington is an easy place to get laid. It's not like I was the prettiest girl in town or anything. I usually wasn't even the prettiest girl in the *room*. But I can tell you that it wasn't my personality that brought all the boys to the yard.

It was a simple matter of economics: supply and demand. Washington lacks those industries that attract the Beautiful People, such as entertainment and fashion. Instead it has the *government*, also known as "Hollywood for the Ugly." And without the model-actress population to compete with, my stock shot up when I moved to DC.

It didn't take much to turn heads there, and everybody was on the make and pretty damn obvious about it. Washington was a town full of young single people and bored married people, all desperate to connect with, oh, anyone. All you had to do was say hi to somebody and they were yours. You could go home with a different man every night of the week if you wanted to. So many men, so little time. How could I lose?

The downside was that almost everyone in Washington was an insecure nerd. Even the better-looking ones had nerdy skeletons in their closets. This was especially true of anyone who worked in politics. Only a nerd would be attracted to *legislative* power, of all things. Nerds love the idea of ruling over people, don't they? They truly believe that they should make all of our decisions for us just because they went to graduate school. I mean, can you name even *one* cool person in politics? There just aren't any. If any of us were truly cool, we would have been living in New York.

I CAME TO WASHINGTON by way of Manhattan, and I had made a nice little life for myself there before I shit all over it. In New York, I mean. And, yes, I suppose that happened in Washington, too, but that was later. New York came first.

We all grew up with big dreams of moving to New York City and living the Glamorous Life, but I was stuck with a four-year scholarship to Syracuse University, while my friends took off for NYU, Columbia, or one of the several "art and design" schools in New York. Between classes at Syracuse, I would trudge through the dirty snow to check my e-mail at one of the campus computer clusters. The brown slush on my practical, reasonably priced L.L. Bean boots would turn into a puddle as I read about the clubs and crazy situations that my friends were getting themselves into in

New York. They were all there, having fun and being fabulous without me, while I languished at keggers and struggled to meet my deadlines at the college newspaper.

I could never get past the feeling that I was missing out on something: I had to get out of Syracuse as soon as possible, before I went insane with boredom.

On the merits of my resume alone, I was granted an interview at Condé Nast Publications in New York. I had beat out countless wannabes (which included many of my classmates at Syracuse) for a highly coveted chance to become a Condé Nastie.

These were the Big Girls: *Vogue, Glamour,* and back then, *Mademoiselle,* the one that hired my best friend, Naomi, right out of journalism school at Columbia. I had known Naomi since the second grade, when we were OshKosh B'Gosh–wearing tomboys who wiped boogers on the other kids when they weren't looking. How cool would it be if we *both* ended up at Condé Nast? I called to tell her the news, and she congratulated me on getting an interview, but warned me that if I didn't "look the part," Human Resources would send me home with nothing but a stack of complimentary magazines.

"Make sure you look good, Jacqueline!" she told me. "Get a blowout and a manicure before you come in. And you might want to tone up a little, too."

I knew that the girls in New York looked like models, but this was a *job interview,* not the velvet rope at Spa. Nevertheless, I had an outstanding resume and a charming personality. How could they *not* hire me?

Obviously, I had much to learn.

.   .   .

"SO HOW DID IT GO?" Naomi asked. We met outside for a cigarette after my interview. I didn't smoke, but I liked to pretend that I did. Smoking looked so good on me. Besides, it gave me something to do whenever I felt like goofing off and standing around outside.

I opened the L.L. Bean Boat and Tote that I used as a handbag, realizing that it didn't look right with the heavy gabardine pantsuit that I was wearing in June. It was the only suit that I owned at the time, and it was all wrong.

Everything about me was wrong: I had put my hair up in a messy ponytail because I was sweating in all of that wool, and my clunky Nine West shoes needed shining, but why bother shining $40 shoes? No makeup, no tan, no manicure: *wrong, wrong, wrong.*

I showed Naomi the stack of free magazines that the Human Resources manager had given me before she showed me the way out.

"They would have given you a *job,*" Naomi told me, "if you had put yourself together like I told you to."

Naomi was wearing a giraffe-print Tracy Feith dress, gold stiletto-heeled sandals, and huge gold bangles on her arms. This was what entry-level employees wore to the offices at Condé Nast. She looked like *Vogue,* she looked like *Mademoiselle.* Naomi looked the part. Then I realized just how dumpy I looked in comparison. I needed a makeover ASAP.

"Did they make you sit in one of the Skinny Chairs?" Naomi asked, but I wasn't sure what she was talking about.

"They have these chairs in there," she explained. "If your ass goes over the edges when you sit down, they won't hire you."

She glanced at my posterior.

"I don't think you fit in," she concluded.

"Too much pizza and beer up at Syracuse," I explained, embarrassed that I was too big for the Big Girls at Condé Nast.

Naomi looked horrified.

"New York girls don't eat," she said. "Learn it. Live it."

# Chapter 2

If Washington's dirty little secret was sex, New York's was its epidemic of eating disorders. *Everybody* had one. It was de rigueur. It was just a part of the Big City makeover that every girl got when she arrived in New York and realized that she needed to step up her game. You start getting your hair blown out and your nails done, and you buy yourself a Kate Spade handbag and a whole new size-zero wardrobe at the Tocca sample sale. When you're done shopping, you have no money left to buy food anyway, so it's just as well.

Not that I was paying for anything anymore. Now that I was thin and gorgeous, New York was the friendliest city in the world: Guys held doors for me, I no longer had to stand on line for *anything*, and it seemed like rich men were always looking for an underfed waif who needed a benefactor.

Why would they be so generous with a girl they hardly knew? Because, unlike their ungrateful wives and spoiled mistresses, I showed these men some *appreciation*. And the nicer I was to them, the nicer they would be to me. It was win-win.

I considered all of this a learning experience. No matter what girl power bullshit you read in *Sassy* magazine, or what your ivory tower women's studies professors at university try to tell you, this world is no meritocracy. It revolves around looks and money. Period. When I was in New York, it was the age of Britney Spears and *Maxim* magazine. You could either miss out on all the fun, or you could make the most of the fact that people were so fucking shallow and take them for all they were worth. Maybe you could even make them see the error of their ways, if you wanted to be moralistic about it.

So I was going out *every* night, and, yes, I was taking drugs and having one-night stands and all that "crazy shit" that young, gorgeous people do. I was unemployed, living in the city that never sleeps, so why not go out and have a good time? I almost didn't *want* to be employed. I didn't want to be one of those dreary people who had to get out of bed at eight in the morning to go to some pain-in-the-ass job every day.

Nevertheless, I once again felt like I was missing out on something. I mean, every time you meet someone new, the first question they always ask is, "What do you do?" I could only be a "party girl" for so long. After I hit twenty-two, it just looked sad. I needed a career, if only for appearance' sake.

My friend Diane hired me for a high-paying copywriting position at an Internet start-up some rich dude had put her in charge of. Of course, they were fucking, so she could do whatever she wanted, and *I* could do whatever I wanted because I was good friends with my boss.

Diane met Naomi and me when we were interns at MTV Networks the summer before my sophomore year. Diane was the one who took us to Twilo for the first time. Naomi and I weren't into the club scene back then. We didn't understand what all the hype was about. Twilo was just a big black room with a disco ball, filled with sweaty people and thumping trance music. If you were sober, it was a living hell. Then Diane gave us our first hits of ecstasy, and we understood *everything*. About a half hour after dropping, Twilo suddenly became Heaven on Earth, and Diane became our new best friend.

Naomi eventually left her shit-paying job at *Mademoiselle* to join Diane and me at the dot-com, so it was the three of us, working and partying together again. We were paid huge salaries to nurse each other's hangovers in the morning and shop for party outfits at Century 21 in the afternoon. And we ran a Web site, when we weren't too busy.

During the dot-com era, there were IPO parties every night of the week on Wall Street. I eventually met my fiancé at one such party. He thought I was a waitress because I was carrying a tray full of drinks, but I was really stocking up before the open bar ended. I gave him a vodka gimlet from my tray, and he gave me a twenty-dollar tip, which I thought was very nice. I gave the twenty back to him, shoving it down his pants. He invited me to his table, and we hit it off right away.

Mike was a boy from Woodside, Queens, a son of a cop who had made good on Wall Street. With his big blue eyes, I found him absolutely adorable, and he wasn't an asshole or a pervert, like most of the Wall Street guys I had met. I felt very lucky to have found a normal guy in New York and believed that Mike was the man I would marry. He was a great catch.

Diane's dot-com inevitably went bankrupt and the rich guy dumped her. We lost our cushy jobs, putting an end to all the fun we were having. The party was over, and we had to get real jobs in the real world. But I was able to put off my job search indefinitely when Mike asked me to move in with him. He paid all of the bills and gave me a shopping allowance, which begged the question: Why bother working when I can be a wealthy housewife?

I had plenty of leisure time to work on my backhand, read every Harry Potter book in print, and try the recipes in the *New York Times Magazine*. Mike took very good care of me. It was my reward for looking pretty, smiling all the time, and cooperating in the bedroom.

I was ready to marry young and retire from the Fly Life. I already had the typical "when-I-was-young-and-crazy-and-lived-in-New-York" experience that included excessive drug use, group sex, crazy boyfriends, and lots of dancing. At this point in my life, cooking spaghetti dinners and renting movies with Mike every Saturday night felt *good*, like I was in rehab or something. I wasn't fighting hangovers every day or waking up in strange places anymore, and I pitied my single friends who still spent their Saturday nights waiting on line for hours to get into Twilo.

But as the months passed, I started to feel like a mental patient, watching television and reading magazines all day. Naomi and Diane had settled down with careers and pseudo-husbands of their own, so I had nobody to go out with anymore. I asked Mike to take me out, but he hated the club scene. He was an awful dancer and drugs frightened him. My nightlife was ruined and it was all Mike's fault. He was obviously robbing me of all the fun I deserved to have as a young, gorgeous female in Manhattan, so I began acting out: I stopped cleaning and the apartment turned to squalor; I quit cooking and insisted on eating out every night; I made him watch *Gone With the Wind* with me instead of the Super Bowl.

I guess I knew that I could get away with all of this because Mike loved me so much, but I was really in no position to pick any fights with him. I had no money of my own, no prospects, and a growing employment gap on my resume. I had no security until we made it legal. Therefore, I had to get him to marry me.

And *what* year was this? Couldn't I get a job? Sure, I just didn't want to. Remember, I had my heart set on becoming a wealthy housewife. Ever since we started living together, everyone kept asking me when the "Big Day" was. Apparently, when you're female, your wedding day is the big moment that your entire life is leading up to. So I waited for Mike to propose.

I waited and waited. Finally, he did, while we were on vacation in the Virgin Islands. (Where he could buy my engagement ring tax-free.) But I wasn't waiting all this time to get *engaged.* I wanted to get *married*: run down to City Hall, fill out the forms, and move on with our lives. But no, we had to plan a wedding, my Big Day. But to me, an engagement was just a way of stalling, and the four-carat ring on my finger was just Mike's way of buying himself more time: time to bail out on me, time to change his mind. I cradled myself in resentment toward him for making me wait.

While I was busy stewing in my own juices, life was passing me by. I hadn't been to Twilo in months. Then the city shut down the club suddenly one Saturday night. I heard it on 1010 WINS the morning after, while I was making breakfast for Mike. It was the end of an era, the official end of my young adulthood. The greatest megaclub that New York had ever seen was closed forever, and I would never drop E beneath its big disco ball again. From now on, I would spend my Saturday nights watching DVDs, going to bed before midnight, and having mediocre sex with the same person. Was that what my entire life had been leading up to?

The months passed, and I was still unmarried, still unemployed. I felt myself getting old, my youth and beauty fading. I was twenty-five years old and had nothing to show for it. There had to be more than this, or I was going to end up killing myself by the time I turned thirty.

So when Kevin, an ex-boyfriend from college, called me unexpectedly, I agreed to meet him, out of melancholy nostalgia.

Kevin and I had had an ongoing flirtation via e-mail since graduation, which was culminating in this visit. Kevin was flying halfway across the country just to see me again. It was the most exciting thing to happen to me in months.

That afternoon, I told Mike I was going to the movies with a girlfriend and then snuck off to meet Kevin at Bemelmans Bar, in the Carlyle Hotel.

After a couple whisky smashes, it was like we never broke up. The piano player provided the usual evocative background music ("As Time Goes By"), and I totally forgot what an asshole Kevin had been in college.

Then he told me that he had a room upstairs with a great view of the Manhattan skyline.

"I'd love to see it," I told him, and I forgot all about Mike.

# *Chapter* 3

I awoke at six o'clock the next morning, naked and tangled in the Carlyle's Frette sheets, hungover and disoriented.

*Where am I?*

*Shit.*

*What time is it?*

*Shit!*

I dressed myself quickly and hurried toward the Seventyseventh Street subway station on Lexington Avenue. I had "conveniently" left my cell phone at home, so Mike wouldn't be able to contact me while I was out with Kevin. But now I couldn't call Mike or anybody else in time to set things straight.

Set things straight? I mean, lie my ass off about where I had been all night.

I got on the Downtown 6, immediately felt nauseated from the movement of the train, and vomited on the seat next to me. Fortunately, the car was empty and nobody saw, or some *stunad* surely would have pulled the emergency brake.

*That would make the perfect excuse*, I realized. I would tell Mike that I was a "sick passenger" (which was the truth), and that I had slept it off on an MTA cot somewhere.

When I arrived at Mike's building, I was very relieved to see that my possessions had not been thrown out the window. I imagined homeless people wrapping themselves in my Diane von Furstenberg dresses and zipping into my Juicy Couture sweatsuits.

I could smell cigarettes through the door to the apartment as I searched for my keys. If Mike had been up all night smoking, that was a very bad sign. (He had supposedly quit when we started dating because he loved me so much.)

"Why does it stink in here?" I asked as I walked in, as if *I* deserved an explanation.

He ignored my question. "Where have you been all night?" he wanted to know.

I went into my sick passenger story, but he stopped me.

"Jackie, please stop lying to me. I called the police and filed a missing persons report. They checked with the MTA."

I was horrified that my one-nighter with Kevin now had an official police record.

"*A missing persons report?* Don't I have to be dead for three days before you can do that?"

"I didn't know where you were!" Mike shouted back. "I thought you were dead!"

"Don't you think you were overreacting?"

"*Overreacting?* I don't know. Why don't you tell me where you slept last night?"

But it was just too awful. I couldn't say a single word, and I didn't need to anyway: He already knew. The police had checked our phone records and called Kevin's room at the Carlyle. Kevin must have freaked out because he turned snitch and told them the whole story.

"How could you do this to me?" Mike asked, fighting back tears.

I never felt worse about anything in my life than making Mike cry. But part of me wanted to tell him that if he had married me sooner, all of this could have been avoided.

Despite what I did with Kevin, I really did love Mike. At least, I loved the *idea* of him: He was the nice, normal guy who wanted to settle down and take care of me.

"I'm sorry," I said, trying to console him.

I walked over to him, expecting to kiss and make up.

"Don't touch me!" he yelled, backing away as if I were a succubus.

The adorable girl he had fallen in love with was dead in his eyes. I knew that he could never look at me the same way again. It was over.

He slammed the door behind him as he left the apartment.

Stunned, I sat down and stroked the big diamond on my left ring finger. We were still engaged, right? We had the kind of relationship that could withstand this sort of thing, didn't we?

Mike called about ten minutes later.

"I think you should move out," he told me.

I could not believe what I was hearing.

"I'm going to my brother's house for the weekend," he went on. "I want you out of the apartment by the time I get back. You have two days. I think that's plenty of time."

Then he hung up.

I sat down and placed my hand on my chest to make sure my heart was still beating. I forced myself to take a deep breath, since I hadn't been breathing the whole time I'd been on the phone. I had no money, no job, no place to live, and the love of my life was throwing me out on my ass. My world was destroyed, but there was no time for cracking up: I had to make a new life for myself in the next forty-eight hours.

Desperate, I picked up my cell phone and dialed the first number listed in my phonebook.

"Where will I go? What will I do?" I cried to my college friend April. She lived in Washington, where she worked for some senator who was running for president.

"You should move to DC!" she suggested excitedly. "You could stay with me! Tom left to work on the campaign, so he's not around. Jackie, it would be so much fun!"

Tom was April's semiserious boyfriend who worked in her office. They didn't officially live together, but I guess she was lonely without him, or else she wouldn't have been asking me to move in with her.

I turned it over in my mind. I had no job, no money, no apartment, no boyfriend, and Twilo was closed. I had no reason to stay in New York anymore.

"What would I do for a job there?" I asked her. "Right now my resume is shit."

"You can get a job on the Hill," she told me. "They're always hiring, just like McDonald's."

Without anything better to do, I accepted April's offer. I FedEx-ed all my possessions (four boxes of clothes and shoes) to her apartment in Capitol Hill that same day, and took the Acela to DC that night.

I tried calling my parents while I was on the train. There was no answer, so I left a very brief and glib message:

"Hi, Mom. Hi, Dad. This is Jacqueline. I'm leaving New York, and I'm on my way to Washington. The marriage is off. Now you don't have to pay for the wedding!"

I had really blown it in New York, hadn't I? Maybe these things happened for a reason. Suppose that I was *meant* to move to Washington. Perhaps it was my destiny.

All I knew was that I would never let this happen to me again. The next time anybody said "I love you" to me, I would laugh in their stupid face.

And I knew that I was damn lucky to have a friend like April, a fun single girl who knew Washington, and could help me get a job on Capitol Hill.

# Chapter 4

That was the plan, even though I didn't know shit about government or politics. I had taken a few poli-sci courses in college, but I had forgotten all of that stuff when I left Syracuse. I had more important things to think about, like finding the perfect pair of hot pants to wear rollerskating at the Roxy. Politics was for dull people with nothing fabulous going on in their lives, who woke up early on Sunday mornings to watch *Meet the Press*.

But if I was going to make a new life for myself in DC, I would have to take this opportunity to learn something new. I was eager to make a fresh start after my miserable failure in New York. This time, I wasn't going to squander my future on marriage proposals: I was going to have a career doing something important, and what was more important than our nation's government?

Plus there's a prestige to working on Capitol Hill that I found highly attractive. I mean, even if I ended up hating my job, wouldn't it look great on my resume?

April suggested that I take an internship in her office while I looked for a paid position on the Hill. Then I could slap a senator's name on my resume, use the office computers to write my cover letters, and start "networking" for jobs. She had referred me to Gloria, the intern coordinator in her office. Despite April's strong recommendation (and the fact that I was more than qualified for a lowly unpaid internship), Gloria insisted that I come in for an interview before granting me entrée into the hallowed halls of Congress.

"WHAT SORTS OF THINGS should I say on my interview?" I asked April as I unpacked the clothes and shoes I had sent to her apartment.

"Oh, the usual job interview BS," she told me, examining each item as I pulled it out of its box. "Where's the other one?" she asked, holding up a single yellow Christian Louboutin pump.

I could see exactly where it was in my mind's eye: under Mike's bed back in New York.

"It's gone," I said, taking the shoe and shoving it into a garbage bag.

"You have nice clothes, Jackie," April said, admiring a red Miu Miu dress from about three or four seasons ago.

"Sample sales," I explained.

Then it occurred to me that sample sales would be a thing of the past from now on. Yet another thing I loved that I had left behind in New York. Where would I get all my clothes from now on? The mall?

"Can I borrow this tonight?" April asked, holding the red dress up against her body. She looked good in red, with her olive skin and long dark hair. I almost wanted to say no, so she wouldn't steal my thunder.

"You can wear that if you want to," I told her, "but I'm not sure if I should go out tonight. I have that interview to-morrow."

"But we have to go out!" April argued. "It's your first night in Washington. We have to celebrate. And don't worry about that interview. Gloria is very nice." She smiled. "Plus you'll get to meet Dan, my office crush."

"April!" I scolded her. "What about Tom?"

"Tom isn't here," she said dismissively. "He's in New Hampshire for the primary, probably fucking the volunteers to stay warm. You know how those campaign chicks are."

I didn't, but I agreed that April should keep her options open. You never know what the other person in your rela-tionship could be doing behind your back.

"I guess I always assume the worst about people," April explained. "Besides, Tom ran away from me to work on the campaign. He's obviously not that serious about me anyway."

"Maybe he thinks your senator will win," I offered. "He's probably doing it just to suck up to your chief of staff, so that he'll get a cushy job in the White House."

"Oh, please! Everybody knows that the senator isn't

going to win New Hampshire. This is just Tom's way of sabotaging our relationship, the way you did when you cheated on Mike."

"*Excuse me?*" I balked. "For your information, I loved Mike very much. I intended to spend the rest of my life with him! He's the one who wanted to end it, not me."

"Then why did you fuck Kevin, of all people? You *hated* Kevin after he dumped you in college, remember?"

"That had nothing to do with Mike. It was just a mistake."

"A mistake? Get real, Jackie. You weren't ready to get married."

"I wasn't? I sure felt like I was ready. I mean, Mike was the perfect guy, and I gave him some of the best years of my life. But even if I *wasn't* ready for marriage, how bad could it have possibly been?"

"Duh, Jackie! Haven't you ever read *Madame Bovary*?"

I rolled my eyes.

"Are you kidding me?" I asked. "I only read the Cliffs Notes."

"You're lucky that this happened while you're still young and hot enough to get this shit out of your system," April explained. "We have the rest of our lives to get married and sit at home anyway. We need to have some fun in the meantime. Let's go out tonight and make out with strangers!"

April wasn't kidding. She put my Miu Miu dress on over a red G-string and matching push-up bra. I finished unpacking and folded up the cardboard boxes I had used to ship my wardrobe from New York to Washington. I would need them again when I packed up again and moved into my own apartment, as soon as I could afford one. I slid the boxes under the sofa bed that I would be sleeping on in the meantime. I hoped that everything would fall into place soon: the job, the apartment, and the strangers whom I had yet to make my boyfriends.

# Chapter 5

April and I met up with Laura, a staff assistant in her office. Getting sloppy drunk and hooking up with strange boys was probably not the best way to make a first impression on a future coworker, but I knew that I could keep myself under control: If I learned anything at Syracuse, it was functional alcoholism. And besides, April assured me that Laura was "cool."

She was a pretty, anorexia-thin blonde who fit in perfectly with the girls at Smith Point: cable-knit Ralph Lauren sweater, pearls, and a Longchamps bag. She wasn't inbred-looking enough to be a genuine New England WASP, so I assumed she was probably from the South somewhere.

"We're the best-looking girls here," she declared as we joined her just inside the door.

The three of us *did* look good together. I could see us going out on a regular basis, making the scene, keeping DC beautiful.

"That's not saying much!" April snorted. "The girls here are *nothing*."

I looked around. Most of the girls here had puffy-looking bodies, with silver Tiffany hearts dangling from their wrists. They clutched bottles of Miller Lite beer and sang along to "Stronger" by Britney Spears.

These girls made their Black Label sweaters look like Polo Sport. Girls drinking *beer*? Out of *bottles*? And what self-respecting woman over the age of sixteen wore those junky silver bracelets? When I *did* wear the Tiffany heart charm bracelet, it was gold, fuck you very much. (A gift Mike had bought me for Valentine's Day one year.)

I excused myself to the bar, ignoring the boys in Abercrombie & Fitch trying to talk to me as I passed by.

If your fiancé ever throws you out of his condo, I highly recommend relocating to our nation's capital. The boys here were so *friendly*, it was almost sad, like nobody ever taught them how to be cool. Like I said, Washington was full of nerds.

But I wouldn't give the date-rapers at Smith Point the time of day, let alone the time of *night*. I had fucked enough of these types back in college. I was a woman now, and I wasn't going back to some GW dorm to make out on a twin-sized bed.

"Ugh, let's get out of here." I returned without ordering anything. "This place is a dump. And I think we're too old. Everybody here is, like, twelve."

"Sit down!" April ordered, pulling a stool over from the bar. "This place is supposed to be fabulous. Laura comes here all the time."

"Sorry this place isn't as cool as any of the bars in *New York*," Laura said dryly.

This girl already hated me. I wasn't sure if I liked her much, either, but she was April's friend and my future coworker, so I had to make an effort to ingratiate myself.

I bought the next round of drinks.

"Girls like us should never have to buy our own drinks," Laura sniffed. "Let's put out *the vibe*."

Laura crossed her legs, tossed her hair, and made eye contact with the only guy in the bar who was wearing a suit. I thought she looked ridiculous, but it seemed to work: He immediately ditched the porcine young lady he was talking to and began his approach toward us.

"Ooh, a young attorney," April surmised. "Good work, L."

"You can have him," Laura offered, "but make sure he buys drinks for all three of us."

"But it's *Sunday*," I reminded them. "I don't trust guys who wear suits on the weekend."

"Jackie, don't be such a bitch," April said, straightening her posture and sticking her chest out.

Laura pulled the bait and switch: She introduced the suit wearer to April and immediately excused herself to the ladies' room, taking me with her.

We returned to the table a few minutes later so as not to miss out on the drink order.

The boy sitting at our table was attractive, but not devastatingly so. You could take him or leave him, really.

"What do you do?" I asked him first thing.

"I'm in grad school," he replied.

"Grad school? So do you have to wear a suit to class or something?"

"No, I'm just wearing it for fun."

"*For fun?*" Laura repeated. "You wear a suit *for fun*?"

We all gave each other a look that said, *WTF?*

"So are you buying us drinks or what?" April finally asked.

"Uh, I don't know."

The question seemed to make him uncomfortable.

"I think you should buy us drinks," Laura said, ganging up on him.

"Why should I?" he dared to ask.

Again, *WTF?*

April invited this loser to sit with us, the prettiest girls in Smith Point, and we deserved free drinks for wasting our time.

"*Excuse me?*" Laura was outraged. "Because you're sitting with us, that's why! Somebody else could be sitting here, buying us drinks right now! I think you should leave."

He left the table in his finery, cursing us.

"You guys, we are *so* mean!" I giggled.

"Whatever," Laura sniffed. "Who does that guy think he is, coming here in a suit?"

She grabbed my Malibu and pineapple cocktail, in need of emergency refreshment.

"I wasn't too rude, was I?" she asked.

"Absolutely not!" I reassured her. "Sometimes you have to be cruel to be kind, Laura. You did that guy a *favor*."

"You taught him a very valuable lesson," April agreed. "If you want girls to be nice to you, buy them drinks. Or go back to your dorm room alone!"

We looked around for some other guys to talk to.

"Slim pickings," I observed as a boy wearing a puka shell necklace walked by.

"I miss my boyfriend," April groaned.

"Me too," I sighed.

"Let's get out of here," Laura finally said in disgust.

She left the bar in a cab, swearing off Georgetown bars forever ("for real this time!"), but April wasn't ready to turn in yet.

"Just one more drink! I'll buy," she offered, which is all I needed to hear, but all of the bars on M Street looked empty.

"What the fuck? It's only ten o'clock," I complained.

"It's Sunday," April explained.

"So? It's still early. Where are all the people?"

"They're probably already in bed."

"In bed by ten? Incredible."

We reached the end of M Street.

"We're all out of bars!" April wailed.

"No, we aren't." I turned toward a large brick building that looked more like a public school than a luxury hotel. "We're right in front of the Four Seasons. Let's just go in here."

"Isn't this where hookers go?" April asked.

"Don't worry, we are obviously *not* hookers."

The truth is, the Four Seasons *was* a favorite spot for women seeking rich men in Washington. I wasn't sure if they were hookers, husband-hunters, or just regular hos, but they came to the Four Seasons to be *picked up* all the same. Since April and I were obviously none of the above, I felt perfectly comfortable walking into the Garden Terrace Lounge unescorted.

"May I help you?" the pretty hostess asked, looking at us suspiciously.

She was the only woman in sight, and the lounge was full of single men.

"We're just going to the bar, thanks," I said, trying my best not to sound like a hooker. (Whatever that meant.)

"This is, like, the best place to meet guys!" April whispered. "Look at all of them, sitting by themselves!"

The Four Seasons on a Sunday night. Who knew?

"But where are all the prostitutes?" April asked. "I wanted to see what they look like."

"Maybe they don't work on Sundays," I guessed.

We sat at the bar, and within minutes, we had company: a venture capitalist on April's right, and a government agency chief of staff on my left.

The chief of staff looked like Kenneth Branagh. He said hello and told me that his name was Fred.

"My name is Jacqueline," I said, giving him significant and meaningful eye contact. (Maybe this guy could get me a job somewhere?)

Fred promptly bought me a drink, which automatically granted him permission to keep talking to me.

"So what do you do?" he asked.

"I'm new in town," I explained. "I'll be interning on the Hill until I find a real job."

"Oh, you're an *intern*."

The way that Fred said the word *intern* suggested a sexualized definition of the word, like it was synonymous with blow jobs or something.

He bought me a second glass of bourbon before I could finish the first. I was back on the Poverty Diet, so I was drinking on an empty stomach. I started feeling very relaxed and friendly (read: drunk), as we continued making small talk.

"So where did you go to school?" he asked me.

"I went to Syracuse. And you?"

"I went to school in New Jersey."

"Jersey? You went to Rutgers?"

"Ah, no, actually. Princeton."

"Oh, yes, Princeton! Right." (So embarrassing.)

I looked over at April. She was already sharing a plate of caviar with the venture capitalist.

"I love your dress," I overheard him say.

That was *my* dress she was wearing. Jealous!

I turned back to Fred.

"So, where do you work again?" I asked, batting my eyelashes, crossing my legs toward him.

He looked at me, picking up on what I was putting out there.

"Why don't I show you?" he suggested. "Would you like to see my office? We could go there right now."

"Your office? Why would I want to see your office?" I asked coyly.

I could guess why Fred would want to take me to an empty office in the middle of the night, and I supposed that

I was down for whatever "Oval Office" wish fulfillment he had in mind.

He told me that his office had a great view of the Mall.

"I'd love to see it," I said and followed him through the lobby as the hotel staff watched us leave.

Oh, the things they must have seen working there. Every one of them could probably quit their jobs with all of the blackmail material they had. But I didn't care if anybody saw me leaving the bar with a stranger. It was nobody's business but our own, right?

# Chapter 6

As I climbed into Fred's Volvo SUV, I noticed something in the backseat. A car seat. For a baby.

*Oh.*

Officially, he was only taking me to his office to show me a pretty view of the Mall, so I didn't feel the need to ask him about the car seat at this point. I was much too drunk to have that conversation with him anyway. So I buckled myself into the passenger seat and smiled at him as he started the engine.

The office building was empty except for the bored security guard who waved to Fred as we scampered by, and I wondered how often he brought girls to the office in the middle of the night.

We played the "office tour game" for a few minutes. He

led me from one room to the next and I pretended to be interested. But I really wasn't impressed by any of it: Fred's job sounded kind of boring. Besides, I was too busy wondering when he planned on putting the moves on me.

He concluded the tour by opening a pair of double doors onto a conference room that was bigger than April's apartment.

There was the view. The Capitol. The Washington Monument. The Lincoln Memorial. Glowing yellow in the dark below us.

Fred stood very close.

I stepped away from him, and he took another step closer, backing me into the twenty-seven-foot conference table in the middle of the room. He leaned in, and I could feel his hard-on pressed against me.

I looked up at him, tilting my face toward his. He kissed me, sliding me onto the table. I knew what was precipitating and did not feel like stopping it. He pulled all of my clothes off, but left his on: He only unzipped. We fucked right on the conference table, like something out of *Penthouse Forum*. I was too drunk to have a real orgasm, but I made a lot of noise like I did. When I opened my eyes, I realized that Fred had fucked me the whole length of the table, from one end to the other.

Not bad for my first night in Washington.

I sat up and looked at the view again. The Capitol. The Washington Monument. The Lincoln Memorial. Still there, glowing yellow in the night, no less beautiful.

It was three in the morning by the time Fred took me home.

I imagined his wife standing on the front porch, waiting for him with a rolling pin. Actually, no, she wouldn't be the rolling-pin type, would she? She was probably swirling a glass of scotch in her hand, frowning and contemplating how she could get back at him. Maybe another shopping spree at Saks? Or maybe she didn't care if her husband stayed out all night like this. It was really none of my business either way.

"Don't you have work tomorrow?" I asked him.

He glanced nervously over his shoulder at the baby seat.

*The baby.* I had forgotten all about that. And so had he, apparently. And it was *his* damn baby!

*His* marriage. *His* baby. Not mine.

"When am I going to see you again?" he asked me.

"I don't know," I said. "You're the married one. It's up to you."

"So you know that I'm married?"

"Well, *duh.*"

Fred laughed, retrieving his wedding ring from his trouser pocket. He put it back on his finger and smiled at me.

"So, tell me, what kind of girl has sex with a married man?" he asked.

"What kind of man cheats on his wife?" I retorted, smiling at him.

"Let me borrow your phone."

"You're not calling your wife, are you?" I asked suspiciously.

"Just give me your phone, please."

I watched as he dialed a number and hit the *Send* button. Then I heard a second phone ringing from somewhere inside the car. Obviously, Fred had just called himself from my phone.

"There," he said. "Now we have each other's number."

These older guys knew all the moves, didn't they? But I didn't expect to hear from Fred ever again. He would surely go home, think about what he had done, and realize that it was wrong.

HE CALLED THE NEXT MORNING.

I answered, hungover and squinting in the daylight.

"Let's get together for lunch sometime this week," he said in that rushed tone people use when they're at work. "How about Thursday, at one thirty? I'll meet you at your place."

I had sort of counted on this being a one-night thing, but now it looked like it might turn into an *affair*.

An affair with a married Washington bureaucrat— hilarious!

I climbed out of the sofa bed and looked around the apartment for April. It was apparent that she hadn't come home last night. Maybe that venture capitalist she met had whisked her away to his mansion.

I remembered that my internship interview was at noon. It was already ten thirty. I needed to put myself together for my debut on the Hill.

My skin was dried out from too much drinking the night before, and my hair was knotted up from too much fucking. I had major work to do.

I put my hair in jumbo Velcro rollers and chose the perfect job interview outfit: a gray stretch wool skirt and matching three-quarter-sleeve top, black silk stockings (no naked legs on a job interview), black crocodile Manolos from last year's sample sale, and my graduation pearls.

No makeup—too trampy. But must do brows. Brunettes should use a *blond* pencil. (I learned that from a *Harper's Bazaar* interview with Cindy Crawford.) I needed blusher, especially when I had a hangover. "Orgasm" by NARS was the best. And I could not leave the house without Lancôme's Définicils mascara. Must comb my eyelashes while I was at it, to get rid of any unsightly clumps.

But that was it. *No makeup.*

My nails were trimmed short, neatly filed, with a single coat of clear nail polish. Manicures weren't required here, as they were in New York, and neither were spray-on tans or chemically straightened hair. Now that I lived in Washington, I could finally let myself go.

I took my rollers out. Total pageant hair, unless I parted it to the side just so, for a more professional look.

*Professional.*

I didn't know the meaning of the word.

AS I WALKED OVER TO the Senate office buildings, I imagined the new life that lay ahead of me. Every morning, I would stroll past the Capitol, just as I was doing now. But I was no tourist—I *lived* in this beautiful city full of pretty shit that our tax dollars paid for: pretty marble buildings, pretty statues, pretty monuments to what a great nation this is.

I could see myself in my little gray suit, running around under the Capitol Dome. Doing *what* exactly, I didn't know. April never told me much about the *work* that people did on the Hill. Listening to her, you would think that it was all Happy Hours and staff romances, like an episode of *Ally McBeal* or something. And the impression I got from watching C-SPAN was that everybody got paid to put on a suit and watch each other give speeches all day. *I could do that*, I thought.

I wanted a fluffy government job that I could start taking for granted as soon as possible. I must have looked so *hopeful* in my Marc Jacobs peacoat, with my hair parted perfectly to the side, on my way to get an internship in the United States Senate. I didn't look like the sort of girl who fucked strange married men on conference tables at three o'clock in the morning.

I found the Hart Senate Office Building and queued up for the security screening. I wondered if I would have to stand in line like this every day as I waited for each person ahead of me to clear. Maybe it was the southern or midwestern influence here, but people were so friggin' *slow*. And no one was yelling or complaining about it. I guess there was no rush to get to work.

I threw my black boarskin Kate Spade bag onto the X-ray belt and stepped through the metal detector.

*Beeep!*

"It's probably your shoes, ma'am," one of the security guards said.

*Ma'am?* Was he talking to me?

"You'll have to remove your shoes, ma'am, and put them through the X-ray machine."

"Seriously?" I balked as a plain-looking girl wearing flats grumbled in line behind me.

How unglamorous. So much for my Hill debut. Frown.

*Note to self: You can never wear Manolos as long as you work here.*

Or I could wear them anyway and use the security screening as an excuse for being late to work in the future! Fabulous.

I returned through the metal detector, put my pumps back on, and immediately felt better. I despised that "taken-down-a-notch" feeling I got whenever I took my heels off.

I click-clacked across the marble floor, looking up at *Mountains and Clouds*, the colossal Alexander Calder sculpture in the atrium. The looming steel mountain and the black metal clouds hanging overhead were so ominous-looking. I had never seen anything like it before .

My phone suddenly went off, its Salt-N-Pepa "Push It" ringtone echoing throughout the marble hall. It was April calling to make sure I was on my way to the office.

"Where are you?" she asked.

"I'm standing next to the big black thingy," I told her.

"I always hated that thing. It's so big and scary looking, like something out of a nightmare."

"Exactly! It's fabulous."

"I feel like shit," she groaned.

"Hungover?"

"Big-time. And I'm still wearing your dress. By the way, people are loving it! The senator was in the office this morning, and he was checking me out!"

"Maybe he'll ask you out on a date."

I was kidding, but didn't these things sometimes happen? At least, it was fun to think that they did.

"I feel disgusting," April continued. "I had to buy a toothbrush at the Senate convenience store when I came in this morning."

"The Senate has a convenience store? Where?"

"It's in the Dirksen Building. And isn't it funny that they sell *toothbrushes* there? It's like they know we're all having one-night stands or something!"

"Do they sell condoms?" I asked. "Because if they don't, they probably should."

"Condoms? Oh, please. No one would be caught dead buying condoms here!"

"Why not? Do senators only hire virgins or something? You would think that they would want people with *life experience* working for them, and that they'd want to keep you all disease-free."

"Shit, I have a call on the other line—fucking constituents!" April groaned. "See you up here soon. Bring coffee!"

I looked around. I didn't see a Starbucks anywhere, so I asked a security guard where I should go.

"Two places: Dirksen or Russell," he said, referring to the other two Senate office buildings. "The good coffee is in Russell."

He gave me directions to a pseudo-Starbucks called Cups. To get there from the Hart Building, I had to take the elevator to the ground level, where I crossed over into the Dirksen Building. Once inside Dirksen, I took the stairs down one flight to the basement level, at which point I circumvented the cafeteria, arriving at the hallway that connected Dirksen to Russell, where Cups was located, at the end of the hall.

It took me about half an hour to find the place, and my phone didn't work in the underground tunnels that connected the buildings. But I had come too far to leave empty-handed, so I ordered two triple-shot skim lattes before going back to the Hart Building, which took another fifteen minutes. No wonder government was so inefficient: It took forty-five minutes just to get a decent cup of coffee!

The wait for an elevator took *forever*, which made no sense since the building only had nine floors. Finally, one arrived. Two men in suits got out. Everybody stared at them, but nobody moved to get into their elevator. A sign above the closing doors read SENATORS ONLY. So I guess those guys were senators or something? They didn't *look* important. All I saw were a couple of old men.

An elevator for us regular people arrived, and we all squeezed into it. When the doors shut, I could see that someone had scratched the words *FUCK YOU* on the inside of the doors. I wondered what misfit would do such a thing in a Senate office building, and if they still worked here.

It was the kind of thing that I might do myself when I was high, but I would have to keep myself in check from now on, especially if I ended up working for some ultra-conservative congressman or something. I had heard that Hill staffers could get fired for just about any made-up reason: There was always some flimsy language written into the employee code of conduct that gave congressional offices this sort of discretionary power. It was usually something like "any improper conduct reflecting upon the Senate office."

Of course, everyone knew the old adage "You don't shit where you eat." But if you worked on the Hill, you couldn't shit *anywhere*. If I was serious about making a career here, I would have to hold it in from now on.

APRIL PUT HER CALLER ON hold when I arrived with her coffee.

"I am too hungover to deal with these crazy people," she whined. "I'm forwarding all of my calls to voice mail for the rest of the day!"

April and Laura were both "Front Office Staff Assistants." They greeted visitors and answered phone calls from crazy people all day long, so basically, they were receptionists with college degrees.

"So what happened to you last night?" I asked April.

"Dude, you dissed me," she said. "You left me alone with that creep at the bar!"

She explained that she was out of cash, so she couldn't take a cab home, and the Metro had shut down at midnight. The man she had met at the bar was a guest at the hotel, in town on business from Los Angeles.

"I had no choice but to go back to his room with him," she said. "I ended up fucking him just because I didn't have a ride home!"

"Shhh! Keep it down!" Laura warned from her desk on the other side of the room. "What if someone overhears you?"

"Oh, nobody's listening," April said. "And if they are, they need to get a real job."

Laura took off her telephone headset and shook her hair out.

"If you're not taking calls, then I'm not either," she said, hitting the *Call Fwd* button on her phone. "I can't believe you guys went to the Four Seasons without me. What did you end up doing last night, Jackie?"

"Jackie fucked that guy she left the bar with," April said knowingly.

"How do you know?" I asked.

"You had the apartment to yourself, so I assumed that you might take advantage. I hope he didn't jizz all over my sofa."

"April!" I squawked. "For your information, we did it on a conference table in his office."

"*What?*"

"We'll talk later," I told the girls.

"So where is Dan?" I asked. "I want to see what the office crush looks like!"

"I'll introduce you to him," April said, "but don't you dare say anything, not even kidding! I have a boyfriend!"

"What about that guy at the Four Seasons last night?" Laura asked.

"He didn't count," April said. "He works off the Hill."

"Just be careful. Fun is fun, but you wouldn't want Tom to find out. He would freak the fuck out. And then you'd have to quit working here."

"That's exactly why I only mess with guys who work *off* the Hill. And if you were smart, you would do the same, Laura."

"But I only sleep around with boys who work over on the House side!"

"Laura is a *bicameral* slut," April informed me.

"Jackie, don't listen to her," Laura said. "She's just jealous that I get laid more than she does because I'm a blonde."

Since April couldn't leave her desk, she called up Dan and told him to keep me company while I waited for my interview.

"Make sure you wipe down the conference table when you're done in there," Laura joked.

April and I rolled our eyes.

DAN REMINDED ME OF A young James Spader: somewhat watery-looking, but oddly attractive nonetheless. He wasn't my type—I usually don't go for a guy with glasses—but he was probably the best-looking guy in the office. By Hill standards, that's not saying much, but I could see how April might start crushing on him, being as bored with her job as she was.

In the conference room we made small talk. I felt like he was making excessive eye contact and smiling at me too much. But, then again, I was batting my eyelashes at him and smiling harder than a beauty pageant contestant. I was preparing for my interview so I was trying to be as charming as possible. I couldn't help it if Dan was susceptible to my feminine wiles.

"You're from New York," he said. "So what brings you to DC?"

I wished I had an easier answer to this question. So I made one up.

"I have a boyfriend here," I told him.

"You do?"

I nodded to confirm.

"But I thought—aren't you living with April?" he asked.

"I'm not ready to move in with him just yet," I lied. "But, yes, I'm living with April for the time being."

What was he trying to say about my pretend relationship with my imaginary boyfriend? That it wasn't serious?

He moved on.

"So what issues are you interested in?" he asked. "What would you like to work on?"

I struck a thoughtful pose, but was unable to come up with an answer. Did I give a shit about anything besides my own wardrobe and well-being? Not really.

"What do you know about appropriations?" Dan asked. "We always need help with our appropriations requests."

*Appropriations.* The word alone bored me to tears.

"That would be great," I said, tossing my hair.

"Great," he agreed. "I'll check and see if Gloria is ready to see you."

I aced the interview; I would begin the next day as an intern. Another day, another no dollar. But now I could put it on my resume and start looking for a real job.


I TRIED CALLING HOME, to give the fam an update, but again, there was no answer, so I called up my sister, Lee, who was away at school.

"Mike broke up with me!" I announced when she picked up the phone. "The wedding is off, and now I'm in Washington, sleeping on my friend's couch!"

"What did you do?" she asked, knowing that this could only be my fault.

"I fucked up," I admitted and told her the whole story, to which she responded with her usual candor.

"Mike wasn't right for you anyway," she said. "He was too nice."

"But that's why I should have him." I sighed. "He was the nicest guy I ever met."

"And then he threw you away! If he loved you, he would have married you by now. And if *you* loved *him*, you wouldn't have fucked Kevin. You probably *wanted* to get caught cheating, because subconsciously, you wanted a way out."

(Lee was a psych major.)

"I didn't want any of this to happen!" I argued. "I ruined everything. But there's nothing I can do now. Mike hates me, and I have no right to bother him ever again. It's over."

"So what will you do now that you have your freedom?" Lee asked. "Are you enjoying the single life?"

"Well, right now I have to get a job, but I'm interning on the Hill in the meantime."

"Aren't you too old to be an intern? It's a little *Strangers with Candy*."

"Yeah, but I don't know what else to do with myself."

"How much do internships pay?"

"They don't."

"That sucks! So what are you doing for money? Are Mom and Dad helping you out?"

"Actually, I haven't heard from them lately. I've tried calling home several times but they never pick up."

"Yeah, me too," Lee said. "It's not like them to dodge our calls."

"Were you calling home to ask for money again?"

My sister was *always* hitting my parents up for cash. And they would actually give it to her, which enraged me. When *I* was in college, I worked as a cocktail waitress, which turned me into the malevolent misanthrope that I am today. I was too proud to beg my parents for handouts. But not Lee.

"Can I borrow some money?" she asked me. "I'll totally pay you back."

I sighed, knowing that she would never repay me.

"I'm broke, but I'll put a check in the mail this afternoon," I said. "If you hear from Mom and Dad, tell them to call me. I'm starting to worry."

"Me, too. They forgot to pay my Visa bill."

"Oh, get a job, Lee."

"Don't be a bitch, Jackie. Just send me a check. And try to have some fun now that you're single again. You need to get yourself a rebound guy and forget about Mike."

I told Lee about Fred, and we agreed that he was definitely a rebound guy: The most I could hope for with him was some hot sex and that was it.

But I didn't want to rebound—I wanted to *dunk*.

"I hate being single again," I told Lee.

"Well, you know what they say: You can either be single and lonely, or married and bored," she offered.

"Thanks for cheering me up, Lee."

I got off the phone and went to bed. Or, in my case, the couch.

# Chapter 7

April skipped her morning workout so we could walk to the office together on my first day. I appreciated the nice gesture, but we kept getting in each other's way, trying to do our hair and makeup in front of the same mirror. I wondered just how soon I would wear out my welcome here.

"Maybe you could get a job as a waitress in the meantime," April suggested, rummaging through my half of the closet, looking for something to wear. "You could work at Hooters or something."

I was appalled at the suggestion.

"I am *not* a waitress," I said indignantly. "My tits aren't big enough anyway."

I checked myself out in the full-length mirror, as I pulled a sweater on over my chest. No, they definitely were not big enough, even though I was taking extra birth control pills to give that part of my body more volume.

I was a fat thin person: a scrawny size zero whose body consisted of bones and flab, but no muscle. April was also a size zero, but she had one of those "gym bodies" sculpted by daily workouts at Gold's. (They gave Hill staffers a generous membership discount.)

She shook her head at me as I put on the mink coat that I had borrowed from my mother.

"What? It's cold out!" I said defensively.

"Yeah, but *interns* don't typically walk around the Senate offices wearing furs," she sniffed.

"I'm not going to walk around the *office* in my fur, April. Besides, who gives a fuck what some intern is wearing?"

"You don't want to give people a reason not to like you on your first day, do you?"

"Oh, please. It's the fucking U.S. Senate. I'm sure people have better things to do than sweat *me*."

"But what if someone throws paint on it or something?"

"Would security actually let someone into the building with a can of red paint? As if."

Besides, even if somebody threw paint on me, I was the sort of person who would wear my fur *with* the paint stains, just to show them that I didn't care. Now *that* would be a fashion statement. I would have been surprised if Alexander McQueen or someone wasn't already selling fur coats with paint stains on them.

. . .

GLORIA GAVE ME SOME paperwork to fill out when I got to the office, including a confidentiality agreement. I wondered what sort of stuff went on here that I had to keep on the D-L? Wasn't this place on the up-and-up?

Then Gloria took me and the other interns down to the Senate ID Office to have our photos taken for our security badges.

"Sexy!" Dan said later when I showed him my finished ID photo. "You look like Catherine Zeta-Jones."

I was surprised that Dan would use the word *sexy*. It seemed kind of inappropriate, but I *did* look like CZJ in that picture. In person, I looked more like the Jessica Lovejoy character from that one episode of *The Simpsons*. But I knew something about posing for pictures: I watched *America's Next Top Model* every week and I owned *Zoolander* on DVD.

On my way back to the mailroom with the other interns, I was intercepted by Kate, the senator's scheduler. Kate, a middle-aged woman who kept jars of candy all over her office, informed me that I would be helping her with "regrets" from now on.

I grabbed my coat and handbag from the closet before leaving the room with her.

"Is that real fur?" she asked.

"It's one of my mother's," I told her.

She raised her eyebrows but said nothing further on the subject. We sat down in her office and she explained that the senator could not attend any events in Washington while he was running for president. So my job was to RSVP to these invitations and send the senator's regrets. Easy enough.

I would have preferred to lie low, sorting mail and goofing off with the other interns in the mailroom, but was nevertheless flattered that Kate had chosen me. I got my own cubicle right outside the senator's office! I planned to buy a bud vase for my desk, just like Mary Tyler Moore.

I noticed that a lot of people in the office kept a "Me Wall" in their cubicles, these little photo galleries of themselves standing next to Congressman So-and-So, Senator What's-His-Face, and Governor Whoever. As if that was supposed to impress anyone. Like, "Wow! You got to stand next to some unrecognizable person who is way more important than you are! That's awesome! Excuse me while I jizz all over myself!"

Kate put a stack of invites on my desk.

"If you see anything that looks interesting, you can ask if the invitation is transferable," she told me. "I go to events on the senator's behalf all the time."

That sounded like fun, but I was pretty disappointed when I saw the invitations. Senators got invited to a lot of lame parties, like receptions in honor of helicopters, and charity balls for revolting diseases I had never heard of (Blue Diaper Syndrome?). Being a congressman must have really sucked sometimes. I would have killed myself if I had to go to all these dumb things, even with all the free booze.

So I was making phone calls, setting up my desk, and typing up a few cover letters for jobs that I was applying to, minding my own business. Then Dan stopped by my cubicle.

"What's up?" he asked. "What are you doing in here?"

"Not much," I replied, minimizing the cover letter that I was working on. "I'm just helping Kate."

"Doing what?"

"Calling people and telling them that the senator can't go to their parties."

Dan looked surprised.

"I thought you were supposed to be working on appropriations," he said.

"Yeah, so did I. What happened?" I asked him, smiling.

"Jacqueline, *sweetie!*" Kate called from her office. "Could I please see you?"

I excused myself to see what she wanted.

"Close the door," she whispered.

I shut the door, curious as to why we needed the privacy.

"Have you finished that stack of regrets I just gave you?" she asked me.

"I'm almost done," I told her.

"Jacqueline," she began, "you are a very attractive young woman, and there are a lot of single guys in this office."

*Oh, no.*

"But I cannot have you *entertaining* them in your cubicle."

*What!*

"You should not encourage any of them to talk to you while you're working," she continued. "Look, I know how these guys are. They'll stand there and talk to you all day if you let them. If you're interested in any of the guys in the office, you should go for it, but I don't want them interfering with your work."

*Go for it?*

"Don't worry, Kate," I told her before returning to my desk. "I didn't come here to meet guys."

Seriously, I didn't.

I was never tempted to date in the workplace, especially on the Hill. Not just for professional reasons, but because the guys here really weren't my type. I always hated those obnoxious poli-sci majors in college, who ran for student government and tried to schmooze me to write up their fraternity's charity work in the student newspaper.

Take one of these bottom-feeders, put him through grad school, sell him a cheap suit, and you had your typical Capitol Hill male. According to April and Laura, these guys watched themselves on C-SPAN when they got home from work at night, bored their dates with anecdotes about the congressmen they worked for, and had framed pictures of themselves with people like Dan Quayle. They wore their BlackBerries *and* cell phones clipped to their belts, and some of them even wore *bow ties*. But worst of all, they made less than six figures, which was so not sexy.

# Chapter 8

I was looking forward to my lunch date with Fred if only because I hadn't eaten a decent meal since New York. I was starving by the time Fred arrived at April's on Thursday afternoon.

He looked around the apartment, which was decorated in her taste: sky-blue walls and brightly colored Ikea furniture, with plenty of junk from Crate & Barrel thrown in. He sat on the red foam couch in the living room without saying a word.

"I hope you didn't expect me to cook anything," I said, breaking the silence. "We can't use the oven because I'm keeping my summer wardrobe stored in there."

I sat down next to him.

"So where are you taking me?" I asked.

"We can't go out to lunch," he told me.

I waited for further explanation.

"We have to be discreet, and I can't risk being seen with someone like you."

*Someone like me?* Part of me wanted to call his office and tell them that the people sitting at the conference table right now should know it was streaked with bodily fluids.

What was he so afraid of? Didn't every respectable married man keep a mistress? I would let him finish saying whatever else he had to say. Then I would run up to him and kick him in the balls.

"Since I can't take you out anywhere or offer you any kind of a future," he went on, "I would feel guilty seeing you if I didn't compensate you in some way."

*Compensate?*

"You mean, like, money?" I asked.

"I'd like to give you an allowance, and whatever financial assistance you need," he explained. "I know that you're interning and you could probably use the money. It's only fair."

I wanted to know how much, but felt it would be tacky to ask.

"Sure," I said. "That makes sense."

At least I knew where I stood with him. No dating, no future. Just Fred and me, and some help with the bills. This was probably the most honest relationship I would ever have in my life.

He finished quickly, and I wondered how much five minutes of missionary was worth to him. But he didn't get up from the bed to leave. He lay next to me, drawing me close in his arms.

Snuggling up to Fred felt unnatural. He was still a stranger to me, and I didn't have "snuggly" feelings for him yet. This was false intimacy, and I didn't like it. It was almost offensive, in the same way that a bad liar insulted your intelligence.

But maybe if he felt this comfortable with me, then I could stand to open myself up to him in return. I put my head on his shoulder and listened to him talk. He was complaining mostly, about his job, his marriage, all the things he loathed about Washington.

I got the feeling that Fred had nobody else to talk to. What he really wanted was someone who would listen to him. (And get him off on a regular basis, but that seemed incidental now.)

I asked him why he lived in Washington if he hated it here so much. It was my effort to participate in the "conversation," which was fast becoming an hour-long monologue.

Fred smiled at me and said, "When the president offers you a job, you don't say no."

I looked at him dubiously. He wasn't kidding.

"You know *the president*?" I asked incredulously. "You're, like, *friends* with him?"

I didn't know if I was more impressed with Fred or with myself. I was just one degree away from POTUS! Damn Washington was a small town.

"That's how I got such a cushy job," he explained. "Not everybody gets to take these long lunches whenever they want to."

I looked at the clock. We had been here just over an hour, not counting our travel time.

He stood up and put his suit back on. Reaching into his jacket, he pulled out a sealed envelope.

"This is for you," he said.

The money.

I thanked him as I tucked the envelope away in my hand-bag. The sight of it made me very uncomfortable for some reason. I supposed I knew that there was something inherently wrong with accepting an envelope full of cash. But then again, what made this any different from letting Fred buy me lunch? Either way, he had to pay. "Because I'm worth it," as L'Oreal would say.

As soon as Fred left the apartment, I tore the envelope open and counted the money inside.

Four hundred dollars. For an hour of my time.

What a country.

Why four hundred dollars? I would never know. We never discussed money, and I never asked any questions; I just accepted the envelopes and said, "Thank you," like the polite, well-bred girl that I was.


THAT NIGHT, I GOT another phone call from my sister.

"Did the check bounce?" I asked her.

"Yes, but that's not why I'm calling," she sniffled into the phone.

I could tell that Lee had been crying.

"I can send another check," I offered, "and I promise that it won't bounce this time."

"Listen to me!" she said. "Mom and Dad are getting a divorce."

I was totally blindsided. My parents always seemed to have a very comfortable partnership, the kind I wanted for myself someday. Now it seemed as if they had been living a lie.

"Where is this coming from?" I asked incredulously. "What happened?"

"I don't know," Lee sobbed. "Neither of them wanted to talk about it. Dad just called, asking me if I wanted my stuff shipped to the sorority house. Hasn't he called you yet?"

"No, I haven't heard from either of them," I said, wondering why they had left me out of the loop. "Why is Dad sending all your stuff to campus?"

"He's putting the house up for sale! Why else would he be cleaning it out?"

"*He's selling the house?* I can't believe this is happening! Where is Mom supposed to go?"

"What about us, Jackie? We're, like, *homeless!* Where will we go? What will we do?"

"I'll figure something out. In the meantime, I'll send you some money."

I got off the phone and cut Lee a check. She was right: We really were homeless. We couldn't just go home to our parents if life ever got too rough. No more safety net—it was all up to me.

Next, I wrote out a check to April. She was very pleased to know that I could make my half of the rent. At first, I didn't tell her where the money came from, nor did she seem interested in knowing. Money was money, after all.

She probably just assumed that I was getting help from my parents, like everyone else who interned on the Hill. It was too embarrassing to admit that I had a "going rate." It was like walking around every day with a price tag hanging from your dress.

# Chapter 9

Fred offered me his "financial assistance" about two or three times a week. At four hundred dollars per visit, I made twice what April took home in her paycheck. But I still needed to find a real job. I couldn't count on Fred to keep giving me envelopes of cash for the rest of my life. This sort of thing was always finite.

April and Laura helped me put together a resume and some writing samples, and they gave me some helpful career advice during Happy Hour.

"You basically just want to kiss everybody's ass so they'll write you a good letter of recommendation for your grad school applications," Laura told me, picking the olive out of her martini glass.

"I don't want to go to grad school," I explained. "I just want to get a real job."

"I've been looking for a real job for months. I'm just biding my time on the Hill until I make my move to the private sector. I have a few interviews lined up on K Street."

Laura named some lobbying and public relations firms that I hadn't heard of, but April seemed very impressed.

"I hope you'll help me get a job as soon as you get hired at one of these places," she told Laura. "I am so sick of being poor all the time."

"Don't you enjoy working on the Hill?" I asked them. "I mean, you didn't come here to get rich, did you?"

"It's a great out-of-college job," Laura explained, "and I love our office, but I'm just kind of over it."

"I'm not sure that we're supposed to stay on the Hill forever," April offered. "I mean, they can't promote *everybody*, so somebody has to leave every so often. They know that we'll get sick of making less than thirty thousand, and we'll leave to make more money in the private sector after a few years. Then our office will promote whoever is still around."

"I'm convinced that it's just a systemized way of restocking the office with new girls," Laura said, gesturing toward me. "Just like our internship program."

What was I getting myself into? Maybe I should have gone back to school instead.

"Talking to crazy people on the phone might *sound* like fun, like it's one big episode of *Crank Yankers*, but trust me, it gets old fast!" April said.

Was that really what April and Laura got paid to do? Counsel psychos over the telephone?

"We get calls from mental patients with phone privileges all the time," April confirmed. "Sometimes they make death threats against the senator, and then you have to get the Capitol Police involved. It's *so* annoying."

"And then we get calls from lonely old people who just want to complain about *whatever* for hours," Laura said. "Some of them call every day."

"Can't you tell them to stop calling?" I asked.

"We can't tell them off, or we'll get in trouble," April explained. "The rule is, 'Don't say anything to a constituent that you wouldn't want the senator to overhear.'"

"Why? Does he listen in on the calls?" I asked.

"No, he's much too busy to deal with constituents on that level! It just means that we have to be supernice to everyone who calls the office, even if they're completely insane. On Election Day, their votes count just as much as anyone else's."

I imagined voting booths set up in mental hospitals, with patients in blue gowns, lined up to vote for the senator April and Laura worked for. A chill went up my spine.

April hadn't heard from her boyfriend, Tom, in over a week. Each of her phone calls had gone unreturned, as did the e-mails and Instant Messages that she had sent him over the last several days.

"I know that he's very busy with the campaign and everything, but he can't be *that* busy," April said. "I mean he has a fucking BlackBerry! There's just no excuse for it. He could at least have the courtesy to break up with me via e-mail, but I guess even that's too much to ask these days!"

"I know that the senator won't win the nomination, but

what if he gets picked as the running mate?" Laura posed the question. "We could all be working in the White House by next year!"

"That's why I'm holding off on the job search," April said. "Just in case something like that happens."

April and Laura in the White House? It was possible. Every few years, jobs and office space went into flux, and there were winners and losers. I suppose that explained the cultlike atmosphere in the senator's office.

It was as if each office had its own congressman to worship, who was both loved and feared by his own staff. As an outsider, I had to wonder what need it filled for these people. I couldn't imagine that the work itself was very satisfying. It seemed like everyone just ran around in circles, not accomplishing anything, from the most incompetent intern to the senator himself.

I supposed everybody else was here to work and learn, just as I was. Only I didn't come here to work *for* anybody in particular. I was here for my own reasons, as a mercenary. But maybe I would find a cause that I could get behind, just like Han Solo eventually did in *Star Wars*. (Like I said before, Washington was full of nerds, and obviously, I was no exception.)

# Chapter 10

The next day, April forwarded me the press release announcing that the senator was dropping out of the race. She wrote:

Tom just called! He's coming back to DC! So make yourself scarce this weekend—we need to fuck!

I didn't really have anywhere to go when April and Tom took over the apartment. Tom shared a room with another Hill staffer in one of those awful *Real World*-esque group houses, so they couldn't go to his place. Now that Tom was back in the picture, I guessed that I would be spending every weekend walking aimlessly around Washington on my own.

I had Fred's envelope of cash burning a hole in my handbag, so I went to Georgetown for an afternoon of shopping. I was walking back toward the Foggy Bottom/George Washington University Metro stop, loaded down with shopping bags, when a shiny black Mercedes-Benz pulled over.

An attractive older man who looked like the omnipresent graying male model in the Brooks Brothers catalog rolled down the driver's side window and asked me if I needed a ride.

What the hell did he think he was doing, picking up girls off the street? Surely, he didn't think that I was a hooker. I looked more like a bag lady.

"Those bags look heavy," he said. "Let me give you a ride. It's freezing out there."

Against my better judgment, I put my bags in the trunk and got into the car. I guess I was desperate for something exciting to happen to me. If he turned out to be a murderer or something, I would stab him in the face with one of my stilettos. At least I would have an interesting story to tell my girlfriends. Besides, I loathed public transportation.

"I'm Phillip," he said, shaking my hand. "What's your name?"

"I'm Jacqueline," I answered, not sure if I should be telling him my real name.

"Where are you going?"

"Capitol Hill."

"Do you work for a congressman?"

"Right now, I'm interning. But I'm looking for a job."

Phillip told me that he was good friends with a few

congressmen and that he could help me get a job in one of their offices.

"Thank you, but you don't even know me. I could be a totally incompetent idiot!" I laughed.

"But I can tell that you're not," he said. "You're obviously an intelligent young woman."

Men always did this: tell a smart girl that she's pretty, tell a pretty girl that she's smart.

"Why don't you send me your resume and I'll make sure it gets into the right hands," Phillip said, giving me his business card.

I directed him to April's apartment and looked around the car for baby seats or any other telltale signs of a family life. The car was clean. No wedding ring, either.

"You really don't have to help me," I told him as he helped me carry my bags to the door.

"I'm the best thing that ever happened to you," he said, kissing my hand.

I rolled my eyes, but I couldn't help but smile at him as he walked back to his car. He was just the most ridiculous person I had ever met. I wondered if this was how he spent his Saturdays, picking up girls in his car and promising to help them. I guess that it wasn't much different from picking them up in a bar.

I opened the door to April's apartment, hoping that I wasn't walking in on anything. I could hear her faking an orgasm through her bedroom door and hoped that I didn't sound like that when I faked mine.

I really needed to get my own place. Maybe I should give this Phillip guy a call.

. . .

APRIL AND I MULLED IT over in the cafeteria during our lunch hour. Located on the basement level of the Dirksen Building, the Senate cafeteria had no windows, but plenty of greenish fluorescent lighting that made everybody look especially unattractive. Cell phones didn't work from here unless you had Verizon (which we all intended to switch to as soon as our existing plans ran out), and there was a large variety of substandard food to choose from.

It was an awful place to spend your lunch hour, but *everybody* was here. You at least did a walk-through, even if you had already eaten lunch at your desk or at one of the nearby "off-campus" restaurants. Like it or not, it was the place to see and be seen during the workday.

Some of the local papers even sent reporters to the cafeteria to eavesdrop on staffer conversations, so the etiquette was to never trash anyone by name. You always referred to your boss as "the senator," and you had to watch what you said about anyone else, in case they were sitting behind you. (And they always were!)

"It's all a little too *Pretty Woman*," April said when I told her about Phillip. "I wouldn't trust this guy. And what were you thinking, getting into some stranger's car? Are you crazy?"

I nodded.

"And I was bored," I added.

"You should have given Laura a call," April said. "She would have loved to go shopping with you."

"Yeah, right," I snorted. "Does Laura even like me?"

"Why do you ask?"

"Well, you know how girls are."

"What, that we all pretty much hate each other?"

"So Laura *hates* me?"

"I wouldn't say that. She just thinks that you're a little arrogant."

"*Arrogant?*" I protested. "I am not arrogant! I just have high self-esteem!"

"Don't get mad, Jackie. She's probably just jealous. You know, Laura is really just poor white trash from Virginia. She would shit herself if anyone found out."

"Why is that such a big secret? I could tell by the way she dresses that she's trying to compensate for *something*. She looks exactly like a 'Prep Personae' diagram from *The Official Preppy Handbook*."

Just then, Laura strolled into the dining room in a Fair Isle sweater and pearls. She spotted us and walked over to our table.

"If we're both down here, who's in the front office?" April asked her.

"Right now, I have a couple of interns watching our desks," Laura replied. "Jackie, shouldn't you be on your way back to the office by now?"

"Yeah, I guess I should be," I said, getting up from the table.

"Great! You can answer the phones until we get back," Laura smirked. "Tell the other interns to go back to the mailroom when you get there."

I resented Laura for pulling rank on me like this, but I didn't feel like staying there anyway. Not with her there.

And I was sort of pissed that April didn't stick up for me

just then. I needed to get some new friends, but how was a bitchy girl like me supposed to find any? The only people who ever wanted to talk to me were horny guys.

It could be worse, I supposed. Who wanted to hang out with a bunch of girls anyway?


WHEN I GOT BACK TO THE office, I sat down at Laura's desk and deleted her computer wallpaper, an insipid photo of herself standing next to the senator. It was a petty, immature thing to do, but I was a petty, immature person.

I was searching Rotten.com for a good "Fuck of the Month" picture to set as Laura's new background when a bunch of men in Hazmat suits walked into the office.

"Uh, can I help you?" I asked them.

"Stay where you are," one of them instructed just as Dan walked into the room, on his way back from lunch.

"What's going on here?" he asked me. "Did you call these guys?"

I shook my head no.

"The two of you need to stay in this room until we say otherwise," one of the guys in spacesuits told us. "Someone in your mailroom found a powdery, white substance on their desk. Your office is under quarantine until further notice."

White powder? You know what I was thinking: *sniff, sniff.* But obviously, it wasn't drugs or whoever found it wouldn't have called the Capitol Police. *Note to self: Never bring your stash to the office. Someone might think that it's anthrax and call the Bio-chemical Response Team.*

They locked the doors and moved on to the other offices in our suite. Horrified, I looked to Dan for reassurance that we weren't going to die.

"This happens all the time," he explained. "Ever since the senator ran for president, he gets more death threats than ever. It's probably nothing."

"That's fucked up," I said. "The poor, unpaid interns in the mailroom are risking their *lives* for the senator, who could not care less. You would think that the safety of his staff might matter more to him."

"Well, what is he supposed to do? Stop accepting constituent mail?"

"Yes, I think that he should. He doesn't read any of those letters anyway. People should know that writing to your congressman makes absolutely no difference. Maybe they would put their time and energy into something more effective."

"But then the senator would have to fire, like, half the staff," Dan argued. "Hundreds of LCs* would lose their jobs."

"Wouldn't the senator like to save the taxpayers some money anyway?" I argued. "He's paying a dozen staffers thirty thousand a year to write letters to crazy people. It's such a waste!"

But what did I know? I was actually trying to get one of these LC jobs, so I was just a big hypocrite.

He sat down in Laura's chair.

"What's this you're looking at?" he asked, nodding toward the computer monitor on her desk.

---

*Legislative Correspondents, for those of you not in the know

*Oh, crunch.*

I had left Rotten.com up on the screen. Now he was going to know what a sicko I truly was.

" '*Fuck of the Month,*' " he read. "What is this?"

"Oh, nothing! I don't know how that got up there," I lied.

"Yeah, right," he laughed, scrolling down to see a picture of a woman with a giant hairy bush. "Ugh! This is disgusting. I hope you're not this hairy!"

"No, I get waxed every month," I said defensively.

"Really?" he asked, casting his eyes down toward my lap.

That was the point where I had to make a decision: Should I put an end to Dan's leering, or should I encourage it?

April already had a boyfriend, but she would be pissed if she knew that I was flirting with her crush. You know how girls are: As she herself said, we all pretty much hate each other.

I rolled my eyes and turned away from him. Playing hard to get was always the safest bet.

He got up from the desk and walked over to where I was standing.

"Show me?" he asked, trying to pull up my skirt.

"Get away!" I laughed, scurrying away from him. "I'm telling the senator!"

Just then the door opened and Hazmat gave us the all-clear signal. After everybody was so excited, wondering if they had anthrax or not, it turned out to be powdered sugar from some cookies that the chief of staff had baked for an office party. April and Laura stumbled into the office with coffee cups in their hands.

"They wouldn't let us into the office, so we went to the

Dubliner and had the bartender 'Irish' up our coffees," Laura said.

"Hi, Dan," April cooed. "What are you doing here? Waiting for me?"

Dan looked at me nervously and made excuses to get back to his desk.

"Oh. My. God. You will not believe what just happened," I told the girls after he left the room. "April, that guy you like is a total perv."

I thought that they would appreciate my dirty story about Dan, but they were disgusted.

"You like him, don't you?" April accused me. "Why else would you tell him that you're *waxed*?"

"And what were you doing looking at that crap on *my* computer?" Laura wanted to know. "You could get me fired for that!"

"Is it really that serious?" I asked. "Who's going to know? I'll take full responsibility if anyone says anything about it: I'm an intern, so I can't get fired."

I was surprised that April and Laura would come down on me so hard. Maybe it was the alcohol that was making them so emotional, or perhaps I was just wearing out my welcome here.

"I think you should go back to your cubicle," April said. "We'll discuss this later."

"Tonight at the apartment?" I asked.

"Probably not," she replied. "Tom is coming over."

I rolled my eyes and went back to my desk. Just then Kate called me into her office:

"*Sweetie*, could I see you for a minute?"

I had come to loathe the sound of Kate's voice. She always had some crap job for me to do, like count the number of knives and forks in the party supply closet or buy new batteries for the senator's remote. And I hated the way she called me "*sweetie.*" (Trust me, she had a tone.)

Today, I had to Autopen a hundred copies of his new book. The Autopen was a machine with a robotic arm that could forge the senator's signature perfectly. I sent Valentine cards to all of my friends signed by "The Senator," and I even left little notes around the apartment for April:

> Dude!
> We're out of tampons.
> Pick some up at CVS? I'll give you $ later.
> Thanx,
> "The Senator"

Sometimes you had to make your own fun at work.

After signing the books, I went back to my desk and checked my voice mail. A week after sending out my resumes, I hadn't received a single callback. I finally broke down and called Phillip, the guy who promised to help me get a job.

"So happy to hear from you," he said. "Just e-mail me your resume, and I'll forward it to my friends on the Hill. We'll have to go out to dinner and celebrate once you get hired."

I knew how these things worked: If Phillip got me a job, I would have to go out to dinner with him and, at the very least, give him a blow job or something afterward.

About an hour after sending my resume to Phillip, I got a callback for a staff assistant position in a Republican senator's office. I had never heard of the guy, but then again, I didn't know most congressmen from shit, except for the really glam ones like Senator Clinton. If the important people on the Hill were better looking, it might be easier—and more exciting—to spot them.

"*Sweetie!*" Kate called from her office again.

She asked me to run an errand, all the way on the House side.

"I'm wearing heels," I told her. "I'll ask one of the interns in the mailroom to do it."

"*Sweetie,*" Kate said, "maybe you shouldn't wear shoes like that to the office anymore."

"But I'm short. I have to wear heels."

"*Sweetie,* when I ask you to do something, you do it."

"Fine," I said, kicking my Gucci shoes off so they went flying into the wall. "I'm going!"

I walked out of her office barefoot. When I got back to my desk, my shoes were on top of my desk with a Post-it stuck to them.

*SEE ME*, it said in Kate's handwriting.

Yeah, right. I wasn't going back into her office, just so she could berate me. I put my shoes on and walked out of the office. Fuck Kate, and fuck this internship. I had an interview for a real job tomorrow anyway. And I still had Fred.

I WENT TO THE NEARBY Hotel George, where he had a room reserved for us that day. We had started meeting there instead of April's apartment because he was afraid of her walking in on us.

I picked up my key at the front desk and undressed upon entering the room. Fred was already there, working on his laptop.

He asked me what was new in my life, and I told him about my job interview the next day.

"Congratulations," he said. "We'll have to celebrate. I'll order up a bottle of champagne when we're done."

Fucking always came first.

I didn't even like champagne, but it was such a lovely gesture, I didn't have the heart to tell him that the smell of it alone made me nauseated. (Too many Dommy P hangovers during the dot-com era.)

"Here's to your new job," he said, putting a glass of Veuve Clicquot in my hand.

I choked it down and asked for more. (Yes, I choked down *champagne*. How spoiled was I?)

"Jacqueline," he said, reclining on the bed next to me. "There's something I want to tell you."

I sat up, intrigued.

"Can I trust you?" he asked, refilling my glass.

FYI: If you even needed to ask this question, the answer was obviously no, but I said yes anyway. I had a feeling that I was about to hit pay dirt.

He started telling me that his wife didn't fuck him anymore, which frustrated him and hurt his feelings. Typical married guy stuff, right?

But get this: Up until a few months ago, Fred had a mistress. Some secretary type he had picked up at The Prime

Rib. So they were sneaking around, having an affair. Fred even considered leaving his wife for this other woman, he was so in love with her.

Then one day, Fred got a phone call from his mistress. She demanded fifty thousand dollars cash from him, or else she was going to tell his wife about their affair. He was heartbroken that the woman he had fallen in love with would try to extort money from him, but instead of paying her off, Fred told his wife everything.

It was a great story, but why was he telling it to me? Was I supposed to feel bad for him?

"My wife is making me go to therapy," he explained, "and I'm not sure that my therapist would approve of this relationship."

*Therapy?* I thought that Fred talked all of his problems out with me. What did he need a therapist for?

"Did you tell him about us?" I asked.

"Not yet," he replied. "I wasn't sure that I should."

"Do you *want* to stop seeing me?"

"No, I really don't. But he says that I objectify women, and I think that this relationship might be symptomatic of that problem."

"Oh, Fred. All men objectify women. It's not a *problem.* It's just what men *do*."

I climbed on top of him.

"Maybe you should stop seeing this guy," I said. "Your therapy is obviously going nowhere."

I didn't want Fred second-guessing our arrangement until I had another source of income. I rubbed myself against him lap-dancer style, and he got hard immediately.

"Doesn't this feel good?" I whispered into his ear. "There's nothing wrong with what we're doing, and *I'll never tell*."

It was scary how fast a man will forget his wife and child, all of his responsibilities, and everything his therapist tells him, just for some sex.

Fred's therapist would say that he "objectified" me, but there was more to it than that. Fred was obviously having a midlife crisis. He was unhappy in the same way that I was unhappy with Mike: He was bored and wanted passion in his life. It was a classic syndrome. Remember *Madame Bovary*.

And Fred really should have known better. He had been busted for cheating before, but he couldn't stop himself when he saw a pretty young thing sitting next to him at the Four Seasons. He couldn't stop himself from calling her, meeting her in hotel rooms, fucking her. He had plenty of opportunities to stop himself, but he didn't want to.

He had never even asked about birth control. (I was on the Pill, but for all he knew, I could have been carrying his love child.)

Fred had everything to lose, but maybe he *wanted* to lose it all. It was possible to be suicidal without actually wanting to kill yourself. You just got so sick and tired of your life that you brought on your own self-destruction in hopes of starting all over again.

I understood because I had been there myself. And like Fred, I wanted to believe that it was possible to make your life better this way. I had to believe it, or why go on?

When the time came for Fred to go home, he gave me

my envelope and tucked me into bed. Could he trust me? Maybe, maybe not. But I was no extortionist.

After he left, I ordered a $300 bottle of Left Bank Bordeaux from the wine list and drank until I couldn't move. I vomited purple sludge into the bushes on the way to my interview the next morning, but I still made it on time, looking damn near perfect.

It's scary how well some people can put themselves together despite their messed-up personal lives.

# Chapter 11

My interview was with Janet, the office manager. She was no softie. She kept cutting me off and tapping her pencil impatiently on her clipboard while I spoke, as if she couldn't wait to get rid of me.

So I was taken by surprise when she offered me the job on the spot. I was to start the following Monday.

I guess Phillip had put in a good word for me, so she didn't need to check my references or anything. Then again it's not as if I needed a college degree to open the mail and answer the phone.

It was a shitty mailroom job, but a step in the right direction. I could call home and tell Dad that he had one less thing to worry about.

There was no answer, so I left a message. I was sure that

my parents would be happy, possibly even proud that I was working for a senator, albeit one they had probably never heard of. But no one called back. I forgot all about it when April took me to Saki that night to celebrate.

WEDNESDAY WAS MY favorite night of the week for going out. You might think that nobody in Washington would want to party hard on a weeknight, but there was always a line to get in to Saki on Wednesdays. Not many Hill people showed up, which was a good thing: We could get crazy and not have to worry about it coming up at work. The crowd was a good mix of rich kids who didn't have to work for a living and party people who didn't give a fuck about their jobs and planned to call in sick the next day.

Laura met us just in time for "White Lines (Don't Do It)." The deejay played the Grandmaster Flash and Melle Mel song at approximately the same time every night. It was a good song to writhe around and look sexy to.

A boy who looked like Ad-Rock from the Beastie Boys circa 1985 put a glass in my hand and filled it with Grey Goose. He and his friends had bottle service at a nearby table, so we gravitated in that direction.

Seconds later, we each had a drink in our hands and a boy's lap to sit on. I had really just come here to dance tonight, but the Ad-Rock boy kept asking me questions like "Where are you from?" and "What do you do?" The crowd and the music were far too loud to carry on a conversation, so I was forced to lean closer to him so I could hear what he was saying. Then I caught a whiff of his breath, jumped up, and started dancing away from the table.

Just my luck. I found the cutest boy in the club and he smelled like he'd been smoking weed and eating Doritos all day long. Dammit.

Laura followed me to the ladies' room, while April made out with one of Ad-Rock's friends, some dude in a suit who had a bodyguard.

"What time is it?" Laura asked, blotting the sweat from her face.

"It's almost three in the morning," I told her, checking my phone for messages.

"Did you get any calls?"

I shook my head no.

"Loser," she said, snorting a line off the mirror in her Chanel compact.

She had pried out the pressed powder that came inside of it for this sole purpose.

"Are you going to the office tomorrow?" I asked.

"Shit no," she said, chopping out a line for me with her Senate debit card. "Do you think anyone here is going to work tomorrow?"

Apparently, the opening of Saki had heralded a huge drop in productivity among the twentysomething workforce in Washington.

"Do you have any more?" I asked when I finished my line. "I can't do one line and just stop like this."

"*Is anybody carrying in here?*" Laura shouted at the people in the other stalls.

"*No!*" they all shouted back.

"Goddamn liars," Laura muttered.

"It's, like, *impossible* to get drugs in this town," I complained. "April and I were forced to do Robo last week."

"A bottle of Robitussin costs what, eight dollars? I should quit doing all this coke and start drinking cough syrup to save money."

Suddenly, we heard April's voice in the bathroom.

"Jackie? Laura? Where are you guys?"

I opened the door to our stall, and we stepped out to meet her.

"Should I go home with that guy I was making out with?" she asked us. "He's a vice president of a bank or something."

"Do you know how many vice presidents you're going to meet?" I asked her.

She shook her head no.

"More than you'll know what to do with."

"What about Tom?" Laura asked.

"Until I get a ring," April said, wiggling her left ring finger, "I can do whatever the fuck I want."

April was obviously drunk, but she deserved a fun night out, too.

We heard the deejay put on "Relax" by Frankie Goes to Hollywood, and we all ran back out to the dance floor. April and Laura disappeared, so I started dancing with some fool who was wearing a tuxedo.

Suddenly, Laura grabbed me by the arm and pulled me over to the bar. She had a boy with her.

"Sean has coke back at his place!" she told me excitedly.

By then, it was three in the morning, and Saki was about to close.

"Sidebar, Laura," I took her aside. "Who the fuck is Sean?"

"I don't know," she shrugged. "Does it matter? He's a guy with coke!"

Laura and I followed our new best friend Sean up the stairs to the exit. We saw April climb into a limo with the vice president she had met.

"A thousand points for April!" Laura yelled after her. "Leaving the club in a fucking limo!"

"Who the fuck takes a limo to *Saki*?" I asked as it sped off to someplace fabulous.

Sean took Laura and me to his duplex on nearby Euclid Street. He had a big glass coffee table in the living room, perfect for doing coke on. We gathered around it, watching Sean chop out some big, fat lines for us.

"Dude, we like you already," Laura said, taking a seat next to him on a black leather couch.

"How *much* do you like me?" Sean asked suggestively. "Because I have some more stuff upstairs, if you want it."

Laura and I looked at each other, not sure if we should be offended or turned on.

The coke was making us frisky, so she asked me, "Hey, Jackie, do you *want it*?"

I nodded.

"Do *you*?" I asked.

We started giggling as we followed Sean up the stairs.

·  ·  ·

SO TYPICAL. HE MADE US snort the coke off his dick. I always felt kind of stupid doing this, but decided it was worth it: It never hurts to make friends with someone who has a lot of drugs.

"So what do you do, Sean?" I asked while Laura did a line.

"Like, tell us about yourself," she said, coming up for air.

Sean climbed on top of me as I assumed the position. "I'll tell you as soon as I finish."

"I'm a bike messenger," he said about two minutes later.

No wonder he didn't want to tell us before. Girls like Laura turned their noses up at guys like Sean. But I *adored* bike messengers. They looked like rock stars to us girls trapped in offices all day, with those big chains around their waists, and the one pant leg rolled up. I creamed my pants whenever one rode by me on the street. The DC bike messengers were that hot.

Unfortunately, sex on coke wasn't. It was fast and vigorous, but the technique went out the window when you were high. And the more people involved, the sloppier it got. Laura kept shunting me aside and climbing on top of Sean, forcing all of his attention on her.

Why did girls have to make everything a competition like this? I assumed it was just the coke that made her act so greedy, but few people were having more fun than us that night, naked, in bed with a hot guy with a tight ass, and high out of our minds.

Then the sun came up.

"I want to get the fuck out of here," Laura whispered when Sean left the room to pee. "Where is my bra?"

"I don't know," I said, shielding my eyes from the day-light with the very bra she was looking for.

"They should make a chick flick called *Dude, Where's My Bra?*" I said, laughing.

Laura snatched her bra away from me, and I pulled the bed sheet over my head.

"I'm serious. I want to get out of here," she said, scrambling to get up. "Are you coming or not?"

"Not," I grunted.

I didn't have to be anywhere until Monday. I rolled over, turning my back to her.

Laura crept out of the room and down the stairs before Sean came out of the bathroom.

"Did your friend go home?" he asked, pulling down the shades to block out the sunlight.

"Yeah," I answered, sitting up.

"Don't get up, pretty girl," he said, climbing back into the bed with me. "I want you to stay."

Again, the sex wasn't very good, but his body made up for it. The boy had *back* from riding his bike all day. And he had tattoos on his arms, on his neck, and on his calves. I hadn't fucked a guy with tats in years, but it was fun to go slumming every once in a while.

"You know, you were the primary interest," he told me afterward. "I didn't really like your friend that much."

Of course he liked me more than my friend: That's what guys were supposed to say to the girl who ended up staying when the threesome was over.

I gave him my number and he promised to call, but

whatever: Call me, don't call me. Sean was hot, but I could never bring him home to Mother.

I TRIED CALLING HOME again when I got back to my apartment. Again, no answer. I was beginning to feel neglected, which was ridiculous since I was a grown woman. But the only man a girl could count on in this world was her daddy, and if even *he* was dodging my calls, I knew that something was very wrong at home. I had no way of finding out until someone felt like picking up the telephone and telling me what was going on.

In the meantime, I had plenty of ways to keep myself distracted.

April came home shortly after I did, her hair disheveled and her eyeliner smudged.

"Why does my makeup always look better the morning *after* I put it on?" she asked, dousing a cotton ball with my Caswell-Massey Sweet Almond Oil. "Do you know if Laura is going to work today?"

"I doubt it," I told her.

"Shit! That means it's my turn to go into the office."

"You're going to work today?"

"Well, we *both* can't call in sick on the same day, and I called in *last* Thursday."

"Do you need any of this?" I asked, showing her the nice parting gift that Sean had given me: a vial of coke, street value of $300.

"Where did you get that?" she wanted to know.

"Laura and I had a threesome with a drug dealer-slash-bike messenger."

April's green eyes widened.

"Are you serious?" she asked. "Did she eat you out?"

"No! We didn't do anything with each other," I explained. "Laura is really pretty bad at threesomes—don't tell her I said that."

"Don't worry, I won't," April said, doing a bump of coke off her finger.

"So what happened with the vice president?" I asked her.

It turned out the guy who April left the club with was the vice president of a small *country*, not a bank—which explained the limousine and the bodyguard.

"He was such a freak. Do you know what he wanted to do?" she asked. "I'm warning you, it's totally sick."

Of course I wanted to know. I lived for this stuff.

"He wanted to put M&Ms in my butt," she whispered, even though she was telling me this in her own bedroom.

*"What?"*

"And then he wanted to eat them!"

"Ugh!"

I fell on the floor, laughing.

"Plain or peanut?" I asked her.

"He had plain ones."

"Did he keep them in a candy dish next to the bed?"

"Oh, shut up, Jackie! It was seriously the scariest thing that ever happened to me. I couldn't understand half the stuff he was saying, but he implied that he could do whatever he wanted with me because he had diplomatic immunity or something."

"But that doesn't give him the right to make you his human Pez dispenser! You didn't let him do it, did you?"

She wouldn't answer.

"Ha," I laughed. "You can never tell me anything ever again!"

"I was scared, okay?" April admitted. "For all I knew, the guy could have kidnapped me, pumped me full of drugs, and dumped my body into the ocean from a helicopter when he got tired of raping me. And he would get away with it because he's a Very Important Person."

"I don't know, April. That seems pretty far-fetched."

"Oh, whatever! Didn't you once say that you had a boyfriend who liked to strangle you during sex?" she reminded me. "There are a lot of weirdos out there."

"It's actually pretty common. I used to think that I was the only one who did this freaky stuff, like there was something wrong with me, that I was attracting all these sickos. But the more people you talk to, the more you realize that *everyone* has stories like these."

April shook her head.

"No, that's not true," she said after doing another bump. "Most people have really boring lives. I really think that we have a tendency to attract weirdos."

"No," I argued. "We just have a tendency to find strange ways to entertain ourselves."

I took off the Heatherette Hello Kitty minidress that I had worn out the night before. My eyeballs hurt and I could feel a headache coming on.

"I think I'm coming down," I said, pulling my Donovan McNabb jersey over my head.

"Then I'm out of here," April said, throwing her Coach bag over her shoulder. "If I talk to Laura, I'll let you know what she had to say about last night. I hope things don't get weird between the two of you."

On her way out the door, I didn't want to burden April with the regrettable truth that it was too late.

Laura came by the apartment that afternoon to discuss.

"I think we need to talk," she said, sunglasses clamped to her face.

We were both fighting coke hangovers, and I wasn't in the mood.

"There's nothing to talk about," I offered. "We were both high as kites and we got carried away. It's no biggie."

"Speak for yourself," Laura said. "I don't want you to get the wrong idea about me. I'm really not the threesome type."

"Well, who is?" I laughed. "Everyone has at least *one* threesome at some point in their lives."

"Maybe where you come from, they do," she snorted, "but where I come from, people don't do things like that."

"Not true! Haven't you ever watched Jerry Springer? Apparently, poor white trash have threesomes all the time."

I knew that it was a mean thing to say, but someone needed to knock Laura off her high horse. No wonder I didn't have many female friends: Girls were such goddamn bitches.

"How dare you make yourself out to be the innocent Southern Belle," I told her. "What does that make me? The Big City whore? Give me a break! We both know what happened last night, so just cut the shit."

Laura smirked.

"Well, I'm glad we finally got it all out into the open," she said. "Now I can go home and get some sleep."

"Good for you," I retorted. "Now get out of here and take your ugly Vera Bradley bag with you."

She walked toward the door, then turned around.

"Jackie, I would really like for us to be friends," she said, taking off her sunglasses. "I hope we can keep what happened between you and me."

"I don't really give a damn if people know shit about me, and I hope that you don't think that having a threesome is anything to be ashamed of, because if you do, then you shouldn't have done it in the first place. Besides, I already told April."

"I assumed that you would. We girls love to share secrets, just not with the world, okay?"

Her pleading eyes filled with tears, and I couldn't help but feel bad for the girl: crying in front of a bitch like me was not a fun thing to do. As much as I would have liked to be, I wasn't made of stone.

"I'd really like to be friends with you, too," I admitted. "I promise not to tell anyone else."

We kissed each other good-bye (on the cheek), but there was something about this girl that I didn't trust. Despite whatever label we put on our relationship, she was no friend of mine. Like I had said, I hardly knew her, and I didn't owe her a thing. I could go out and get drunk with her, but that was about it. Such was the nature of most friendships in DC, I supposed.

# Chapter 12

M y new office was in the Russell Building, the oldest of the three Senate office buildings. Unlike the more modern offices in Hart and Dirksen, the Russell offices had these awkward, old-fashioned floor plans. The staff was divided into seven separate rooms along the same side of a corridor. Moving from one room to another was like switching classes in school.

My desk was in "the Locker Room," an office full of male staffers. Unfortunately, they were all unattractive. (Fat and/or beard and/or bald.)

On my first day, they were overheard (by me) debating which strip club had the best lunch buffet in DC.

If my officemates liked to jizz inside their pants during

their lunch hour, that was their business. I mean, sometimes I had actual sex during *my* lunch hour, but nobody wanted to hear about that, did they?

"Maybe you guys should IM each other about this stuff," I suggested.

"We shouldn't have to do that just because *you're* in here," one of them (fat, beard) told me. "Whatever happens in the Locker Room stays in the Locker Room!"

Since when did a Senate office become the new Las Vegas?

I guess anything goes here.

After lunch, Janet pulled me out of the mailroom to meet my new boss, the senator. We had to catch him in the hallway between appointments because he didn't do "sit-downs" with anyone from out of state. (I didn't have any votes behind me.)

So this was my one chance to make a good impression. Janet introduced me, giving him a brief summary of my job description.

He stared at my tits the whole time.

Even as we shook hands, he stared at them, and they weren't even that big or anything.

"Sorry about that," Janet whispered as he walked away. "The senator is a horny guy."

I returned to my desk and e-mailed the story to my girl-friends right away.

April wrote back:

you should send this to blogette!

Blogette.com was our favorite Washington gossip site, written by some cool girl who made fun of everybody. This was exactly the sort of material she was posting at the time, but I wasn't about to risk my job and embarrass my office just to give Blogette material for a few cheap jokes.

I TOLD THE STORY TO Phillip over dinner later that week. Maybe he would tell his friend to show some restraint. Horny or not, couldn't he control himself for those few seconds? He was a *senator*, for crying out loud.

"I lost all respect for him after that," I told Phillip. "Not that I had any for him to begin with. Did you know that he's pro-life and shit?"

"Remember to behave yourself in that office! I recommended you to them," Phillip reminded me. "I don't want to hear any complaints about you."

I downed the martini he had ordered for me. He was trying to get me drunk, gesturing to the waiter for another round, and it was working.

This was my first time at The Prime Rib, a fat-cat restaurant on K Street that was popular with lobbyists with big expense accounts. If not for the hideous drop ceiling, it would have been a very handsome place, with its chic black walls and leopard-print carpets.

Pretty office girls sat at the bar, waiting for rich guys to buy them drinks. A few of them tossed their hair and crossed their legs, trying to catch Phillip's eye. He looked very handsome in his pinstripes, French cuffs, and Tiffany cufflinks.

Everything about him said, "I have buttloads of money— come and get it!"

I guessed that he was pushing sixty, which made him the oldest man I had ever dated. At his age, he knew a few things about women. At least, he knew what they wanted to hear.

"Is there anything you'd like me to buy for you?" he asked me.

"Sure, lots of things," I replied. "I'm only making twenty- five thousand dollars a year, you know."

"I put a few of my girlfriends through law school, and I bought the last one a condo," he bragged. "Anything you want, just name it. Jewelry? A car?"

"That's very generous," I said, resisting the urge to laugh, "but I hardly know you."

"That's just the kind of guy I am. And you're a beautiful woman. You deserve to be happy."

"Whatever," I said, rolling my eyes. "You are so full of it."

It was all bullshit until he proved otherwise. Even drunk, I knew the rules. You were supposed to fuck the guy *after* you got him to buy you the condo or whatever. But I never did it that way. Sex came first, and if he liked me, he would deliver. If he didn't, then at least I gave it a shot. It wasn't the most lu- crative way to operate, but if I wanted to be pragmatic I would have just worked as a call girl.

OF COURSE, PHILLIP HAD a house in Georgetown, and it had the crystal chandeliers, oriental carpets, and mahogany furniture that all "rich guy" houses were supposed to have. It was generic-looking, like a movie set.

He served me the most vile-tasting cocktail, which only tasted better the more I drank of it.

"Are these real?" he asked, groping my breasts.

"How dare you!" I laughed, swatting away his advances. "Are *you* for real?"

I gagged my drink down as fast as I could. That way I could tell myself, *I'm not a slut, I was just drunk* when I looked at myself in the mirror the next morning.

I took off my dress and sat down. He stood in front of me and pulled out the biggest dick I had ever seen in my life. Thank God I was drunk, 'cause this was going to hurt.

Luckily I had no gag reflex when I was drunk, so I could take the whole thing down my throat easily.

This was how you made a man with a huge penis fall in love with you. You had to give them what they had been waiting for all their lives: a *real* blow job. They didn't want or need any more halfway blow jobs in their lives. And, no, they didn't want you to use your hands. You had to use your head. (But not for thinking.) Actually, the less you thought about it, the better. And if he ever wanted me to do this for him again, he would buy me anything I wanted in the future.

So that was my first date with Phillip. He got me a job, so I gave him one in return. And they both sucked.

MY JOB WAS TO READ AND sort the constituent mail. At first I found the letters amusing. Some of them were so hilarious, I thought that they might make a good coffee table book someday. But soon I just wanted to save everybody the trouble and throw them all in the trash.

I probably should have quit this job, given someone who cared a shot at all this glory, but I couldn't bail out on April. She needed help with the bills. Besides, I was always too hung-over to make a decision either way.

I opened the first letter from the stack on top of my desk. It was from out of state, so I tossed it. The next three were form letters, so I tossed those out, too.

I tried another one.

> *Dear Senator,*
> *I am OUTRAGED over Janet Jackson's performance*
> *at the Super Bowl Halftime Show . . .*

Another one of these. I added it to the pile. I guess people get outraged pretty easily in the Midwest. I entered the person's name and address into the database, and five weeks later, she would receive a form letter with the senator's signature Autopenned on it. Our tax dollars at work. Seriously, I didn't know why we all didn't just shoot ourselves.

The only good thing about working there was that I could still meet April for lunch in the cafeteria every day.

"Just try not to get fired. And don't quit, either. We need to make rent," she said, flipping through the classifieds section in the back of *Washingtonian* magazine.

"What are you reading the personal ads for?" I asked, peering over the table.

"Are you kidding? The personals are the most interesting part of the magazine. Listen to this: *Married white male, 55, in search of slender female, 18 to 25, for mutually beneficial relationship. Must be discreet.* There's, like, a whole page of ads like these!"

"Wow, that's depressing. I can't believe that the *Washingtonian* would print that stuff. I thought it was a magazine for soccer moms or something."

"If these married guys really want to find some needy young women, they should advertise in *Roll Call*. There are plenty of them on the Hill. Maybe I should write to one of these guys."

"Oh, April, don't! I'm sure they're all serial killers with grudges against women or something," I surmised. "Besides, if you want a man to give you money, all you have to do is ask."

"Yeah, right," she snorted.

"Well, it's not hard to meet a rich guy in DC. I've only been here a short while, and I already have Fred *and* Phillip paying my rent every month. It's the oldest trick in the book, but apparently, it still works."

"Yeah, but you're *fucking* them," April whispered. "It's hooker money."

"It's an *allowance*," I reminded her. "And don't be mad just because you're still going Dutch with Tom."

April huffily grabbed her tray and stood up from the table. She could be such a drama queen sometimes.

"If you think I'm jealous of you, you're crazy," she said. "At least I *have* a boyfriend."

April left me to finish eating my lunch alone like a loser. But I was too self-conscious to sit by myself, so I threw my lunch away and started back toward my office.

On the way back, I ran into Dan. It was the first time I had seen him since I left his office.

"How's the new job?" he asked me.

"Good," I lied.

(Why be a bummer? No one wanted to hear the truth anyway.)

"I want to hear all about it," he said. "Do you want to get a drink after work?"

"Sure," I replied. "Where do you want to go?"

"Let's go to Lounge 201. I get off at six."

"When you get back to the office, ask April if she wants to come," I suggested before we went our separate ways.

Despite our little tiff this afternoon, she would surely be down for some drinking with Dan. If she wanted, I could cut out of there and leave the two of them alone together.

LOUNGE 201 WAS THE MORE "upscale" bar on the Senate side of the Hill. The drinks were priced slightly higher here, to keep interns and other lowlifes away. April and Laura came here frequently to "network," but it was my first time here.

I walked in alone, still wearing my Senate ID badge. I took it off immediately, noticing how *canine* everybody looked walking around with their security badges around their necks. People in DC never seemed to take them off. It was pretty tacky, but at least it gave everyone here a point of reference. All you had to do was read their tag, and you had a person's name and place of employment. If a guy ever got out of line, you could call his office and embarrass the hell out of him the next day.

April and Dan weren't there yet, so I sat at the bar and ordered a glass of red wine. (Good for the skin.)

"You're already drinking," Dan said when he arrived. "That's my kind of girl."

April wasn't with him.

"She said she was going somewhere with Tom," Dan told me. "Sorry I couldn't convince her to change her mind."

"No, that's okay," I said. "We'll have fun without her."

Dan told me that he was meeting up with friends else-where later, which immediately put me at ease. He was al-ready making excuses to ditch me, which meant that he wasn't trying to pick me up. We were just two Senate staffers having a friendly drink together after work.

"How's Kate?" I asked.

"She's still there," he said dryly. "Did you like working with her?"

"Not so much," I said, remembering how she accused me of "entertaining" male staff in my cubicle.

"Kate was pissed about the shoe thing."

I rolled my eyes.

"She's such a bitch," I scoffed.

"Everybody hates Kate," Dan said. "But I thought what you did was awesome. It's, like, legend around the office."

I laughed at this.

"Your presence there is missed," Dan said. "Especially when you wore those low-cut dresses to the office. There was always a lot of, uh, *commentary* among the male staff whenever you walked by our desks."

"Those were *wrap* dresses," I pointed out. "You know, Diane von Furstenberg? They're, like, classic."

"Whatever. They really showed off your rack."

"You're too much," I said, blushing.

I always liked people who could say what was on their mind. Yeah, Dan was a lech, but he was good-looking, so on him, it was endearing.

He went to the bar to buy another round, and I quickly reapplied my NARS lipstick.

"I wish you hadn't gotten hired away from our office so fast," he said, setting our drinks down on the table.

We smiled at each other.

"It's too bad you have a boyfriend," he went on. "I wanted to ask you out. So, are you still with him?"

I remembered I had lied about having a boyfriend the day I got hired. I didn't have one now, and I didn't have one then. I had Fred and Phillip, but neither of them was my *boyfriend* per se. I wasn't even sure what I would call them.

"I'm dating around," I said.

"Dating around? What does that mean?"

I finished my drink in one swallow.

"That means I'm going home with you tonight," I told him, "after we have another drink."

I gave him my empty glass.

"I knew that you would be fun to hang out with," he said before going back to the bar to get me another drink.

I guess he didn't have to leave so soon after all.

"So did you want to fuck me the moment we met or what?" he asked when he returned.

I nearly spit out my wine.

"Oh, *whatever*! Speak for yourself!"

"You're so *vivacious*," he said, putting his hand on my thigh.

*Vivacious?* It was a lame come-on, but yes, I suppose that I was.

"I can tell I'm going to have a lot of fun with you," I told him as we left the bar.

Sure, I was going to fuck him. But there was no way in hell that I wanted to *sleep* with him. Like I would want to snuggle up to an arrogant douchebag who made $30K a year!

# Chapter 13

It was hard to believe that Dan was thirty-five years old. He lived in a sparsely furnished studio apartment that looked more like a dorm room. (This was common among men who spent too much time at graduate school.) There were piles of dirty clothes everywhere, and no place to sit down except for on his bed. I suspected that Dan kept it this way to facilitate hookups like these.

Once I was on the bed, he turned the lights off and sat down next to me.

I started removing my clothes, putting an end to any pretense as to what we were doing here.

"I've been dreaming about this for months," he said, climbing on top of me. "I've been wanting to do this ever since we met."

"Really? I had no idea," I lied.

We fucked missionary for a little while, but it didn't seem to satisfy him. He flipped me over in the doggie position, and we did that for a few minutes. Then he did something very interesting: He slipped out of Door Number One and tried to sneak into Door Number Two.

So, the anal thing: Since when did it become de rigueur? I mean, for us heterosexuals? I guess we figure we have some catching up to do. If gay men did it all the time, I was determined to prove that I could take it like a man.

"If you want to do *that*, we'll need lube," I told him.

I sort of hoped that he didn't have any so I'd have an excuse to deny access. But Dan was a single guy, so of course he had a bottle of Astroglide. And it looked like a new bottle, as though he had bought it in anticipation of such an event. (But if he was expecting company, why not tidy the apartment up a little?)

Of course, I had reservations about letting someone from work butt-fuck me, but if he was game, so was I.

But it wasn't enough for Dan.

"Hey, let's do it in front of the mirror," he suggested.

I looked around the room.

"What mirror?"

"In the bathroom."

At this point, why not? At least he kept his bathroom clean.

In front of the sink, leaning over, I noticed that he used a lot of hair and skincare products, even more than I did. And the way he kept looking at himself in the mirror while he fucked me, I could tell this guy was pretty damn narcissistic.

He finished, but I couldn't be sure if it was *me* that did it for him, or if I was just there so he had something to fuck while he admired himself in the mirror. Either way, it was all pretty funny, and the girls were going to piss themselves laughing when I told them about it tomorrow.

The wine I drank at 201 hit me as soon as I lay down. Dan was fawning over me, stroking my hair, kissing the back of my neck. It would have been very romantic if I hadn't felt so nauseated.

"I should leave," I said, trying to get up.

"Don't go, don't go," Dan said, holding me.

At the time, these sounded like the most beautiful words I had ever heard.

WHEN I CAME TO, DAN was awake, still in bed with me. He had been watching me as I slept.

*What a creep,* I thought.

"You're pretty when you're sleeping," he told me.

And I'm ugly when I'm awake?

"Whatev," I replied.

"Am I the first guy on the Hill that you've had sex with?" he asked.

"Yeah," I lied. "Why do you ask?"

"How many people have you slept with?"

"Since I got here, or in my lifetime?"

"Lifetime."

"Not that many. Like, eleven or twelve. What about you?"

"Six or seven."

I started laughing.

"*Six or seven?*" I asked. "I hope you're lying!"

"No, really," he insisted. "I don't sleep around."

What world was he living in? Did he really want me to think that this was *special* for him or something? He obviously thought I was simple.

"Of those eleven or twelve guys that you've slept with, where do I rank?" he asked me. "Top five?"

"Jesus, I don't know," I replied. "What do you want me to say? That you're the best I've ever had?"

Of course, I knew that was *exactly* what Dan wanted to hear. People had sex for two reasons:

1. To have an orgasm.
2. To hear someone say nice things to them.

He stretched himself out on the bed, showing off the huge morning hard-on that he had, as if it were so irresistible that I'd want to jump on top of him. I thought about it, but I started putting my clothes back on instead. I got more satisfaction from turning him down than I ever could from fucking him.

"Why are you getting dressed?" he asked.

"I have to get going," I told him.

"No, you don't," he said, pulling me toward him.

I looked into his eyes.

He didn't get it, did he? Did he really think that I would let myself be loved by a jerk like him?

"I really have to go," I repeated. "I have stuff to do today."

I backed away from the bed and finished getting dressed.

"I'll see you around," I said, leaving him alone in his slovenly apartment.

. . .

APRIL WAS UP DOING laundry when I came home. I was secretly happy that Tom wasn't here for once, so I could give her all the dirt on Dan.

But she was not amused by my story.

"That is so skanky," was her indignant response.

"Oh, dude, do you care?" I asked her. "Don't make me sorry that I told you."

"Jackie, you really need to stop having sex with people who don't care about you," she sniffed.

"Well, it's not as if I care about him, either," I replied defensively. "I hardly even know the guy."

"That's exactly my point. I hope you know that Dan has a reputation for hooking up with interns in our office."

"So I'm just one of the many Capitol Hill sluts who has jumped into bed with Dan," I said. "What's the big deal?"

"I'm just very disappointed in the both of you."

April was acting pretty uppity for someone who let strangers put candy up her ass. Obviously, she was jealous that I got to fuck her crush before she did.

"I didn't mean for this to happen," I tried to explain. "Maybe if you had answered my Instant Messages yesterday afternoon, you would have cancelled your plans with Tom and hooked up with Dan yourself."

"What the fuck are you talking about?" April asked. "I didn't have plans with Tom."

"I told Dan to invite you out for drinks after work, but he told me that you had a previous engagement."

"Dan never asked me out for drinks," April said. "That asshole! I'm going to call him right now!"

"And tell him what? That you're mad because he had sex with me? Please!"

She ignored me and dialed his number.

"He's not picking up," she said after a few rings and hung up without leaving a message.

Then *my* phone rang. It was Dan. I went outside to take the call so that April couldn't overhear.

"I was just calling to make sure everything is okay," he said. "April just tried to call me. Did you tell her anything about us?"

"She's my roommate," I reminded him.

"Look at it this way," he said. "If you can't keep a secret, what makes you think that anybody else can? I just don't want any trouble at work. You know how people like to talk."

He had a point. But why did everything have to be a secret? If Dan was worried about his reputation, he should have been more careful about who he took to bed with him.

I went back into the apartment to set things right with April.

"Are you mad at me?" I asked her. "I hope not, because Dan is not worth fighting over. I'm sorry I made out with him."

"Forget about it," she said. "You and Dan can do whatever you want. I have a boyfriend, and I shouldn't have been crushing on other guys anyway. If you want him, you can have him."

"Uh, thanks," I replied, "but I don't really want him, either. He just called me, talking about, 'let's keep it a secret.' What a scrub."

"Yeah, but you'll still have to see him at work," she reminded me.

Damn, I forgot about that.

"What if I run into him in the cafeteria, or in the hall?" I fretted. "What if he sees me talking to other boys?"

"What if you see him talking to other girls?" she asked.

It was junior high all over again.

BACK AT WORK ON Monday, I e-mailed the story about Dan to Naomi and Diane in New York. I felt sort of weird about forcing this bullshit into their in-boxes, but they IM-ed me back with all sorts of questions about what happened.

> how big was it?
> did he go down on you?
> six or seven? is he ugly or something?

Obviously, I wasn't getting much work done. By the time we finished, it was almost noon. Time to go to the hotel to meet Fred.

# Chapter 14

"I don't know if we can keep meeting here," he said when I slipped into the elevator behind him. "I just saw someone from the office in the lobby. The son of a bitch asked me what I was doing here when he saw me checking in."

"What was *he* doing here?" I asked. "Probably the same thing."

"He was having lunch at the restaurant downstairs, actually."

"So what did you tell him?"

"That I needed to take a nap."

"Oh, that's an awful excuse. You should have just told him the truth, if he thinks you're up to something anyway. He probably would have been more impressed."

Fred unlocked the door to our room and let me in ahead of him.

"Have you thought about getting your own apartment?" he asked. "It would be better if we could meet someplace private."

I had wanted to get my own place ever since I moved to DC, but I could never save any money. Even with all the extra income that Fred provided, I never had more than a few hundred dollars in my bank account.

As I undressed, I told him about my money woes and my mean roommate who was making my life miserable. Then I turned on the tears.

"Just find a nice place, and I'll write you a check," he promised.

It worked every time. I didn't even need to ask. I kissed and hugged him to show him how grateful I was, then he carried me over to the bed and took it out in trade.

Because I was worth it.

WHEN I GOT BACK TO THE Locker Room, my officemates complained that my phone had been ringing nonstop while I was out. I checked my voice mail, but there was only one message. It was from Dan, who wanted to go out to lunch this afternoon, but he was too late.

The phone rang again, but I didn't recognize the number on my caller ID, so I didn't pick up. Following a hunch that I had, I looked up Dan's number in the Senate directory, and it was a match.

He called back a few times that afternoon without leaving

any messages. I guess he didn't want to look desperate. Too bad he didn't know that I had caller ID, so I knew how crazy about me he really was.

This went on all week long. (My officemates wanted to kill me.) I didn't want to answer the phone because I didn't know how to act toward Dan. At first, I thought that he only wanted to use me for sex, which was fine with me since the feeling was mutual. I mean, all that raunchy behavior sort of set the tone.

But what was up with all of these phone calls? Fuck buddies weren't supposed to sweat you that hard. It seemed as though Dan might actually *like* me.


I DIDN'T HAVE TIME TO figure this guy out, especially now that I was in the middle of an apartment search. I found a newly finished English basement near Eastern Market, clean and freshly painted, unlike all the other places I had seen. I was tired of looking at dumpy studios with dirty floors and ugly kitchen cabinets, so I took it right away, even though there was no way I could afford it on my own. But this pretty one-bedroom fit the lifestyle I imagined for myself so much better, and I had both Fred and Phillip wrapped around my pretty little finger.

Of course, I had terrible credit, so I convinced Phillip to sign the lease during one of our preintercourse cocktail hours at his place. Sure, he was drunk and horny, and it was probably wrong to take advantage of him the way I did, but if he really cared about me, he would have signed it anyway, right?

Moving was easy since I didn't have any furniture of my own. Fred actually got away from his wife for a few hours to help me pick up my new bed in his SUV. He told her that he was playing eighteen holes up at Burning Bush that afternoon.

I guess that was why so many men took up golf: It gave them an excuse to get away from their wives and run errands with their girlfriends.

April didn't know whether to be happy that I was finally moving out of her apartment or pissed that I was doing so on such short notice. Women! I don't know how men put up with us.

Oh, that's right: *sex*. Otherwise, what good were we?

"Maybe now that I'm moving out of your apartment, you can ask Tom to move in," I suggested to April over lunch.

"Get this," she said, "he says he's going to propose 'sometime this fall.' How fucked up is that? I just want to get married, the sooner the better. I'm sick of being poor. I'm sick of sleeping around. I just want to get it over with."

It was always frightening to hear somebody talk this way about marriage. *I just want to get it over with.* That's what suicidal people would say. Marriage. Suicide. Same difference. Either way, you could say good-bye to your friend.

"If you're in a hurry to get married, you should just get pregnant," I offered. "And you know that Tom wouldn't make you get an abortion because your senator is pro-life. Ha!"

April thought on this.

"Isn't it incredible that women have so much power to utterly wreak havoc on men's lives?" she marveled. "And men can't do shit about it?"

"They can beat us up," I said. "They're bigger than we are."

"Well, that's what jail is for. But it's not illegal to get pregnant and mess up someone's life? There ought to be a law."

"April, we're in the right place. You should bring it up with your senator first thing when you get back to the office!"

"I'm serious, Jackie!"

I shrugged.

"Most of the men I know are totally oblivious, or else they would be more careful," I told April. "They say and do things that you just *shouldn't* say and do to a stranger. I don't know if they're crazy or lonely or what."

"They think that you don't have any power," April surmised. "To them, you're just an object."

"An object?" I asked, getting up from the table. "Well, that's *their* mistake."

I had to get back to my desk in time to catch *Law & Order*. I hurried up the stairs and down the hall toward my office. Just then, I saw the senator step out of his office on his way to the gym, according to his official schedule. (He really went there just to take naps during the day.)

"Hi," I said to him as we passed in the hallway.

He looked at me blankly and kept right on walking.

He could have at least nodded or something, but it was obvious that he had no idea who I was. I guess when Janet introduced us, all he saw was a new pair of tits.

I watched *L&O* and did some work until the office closed at six. On the way over to the Hart Building, some random dude from one of the committee offices tried to pick me up, but I already had plans for the night.

Dan was waiting for me under *Mountains and Clouds* in the atrium.

"Where are we going?" I asked him.

"Let's go to your place. You live closer," he said.

Well, why not? I had about six hours between the time I got off work and the time I went to sleep. What was I going to do with all that time? Call me crazy, but drinking and fucking seemed like a good way to pass the hours.

We stopped at a bar on the way to my apartment, so that Dan could feed me enough alcohol to get me in the mood. Sex was always so much more fun when I was drunk. Any freaky thing that the guy wanted to do seemed like a great idea, even breaking into the Senate offices to have sex on his desk.

"We could go there right now," Dan said. "I have a key."

What was it about sex in the office that men loved so much? I wondered how many staffers were sneaking into the buildings at night to get it on. All of us had keys, and there were so many rooms, so many desks. How could we *not* do it?

The Capitol Police let us into the Senate complex even though we were obviously up to no good. I stopped to examine the security log that Dan and I had signed in our most illegible penmanship. There were at least a dozen other people who probably had the same idea as we did. Some of them were still somewhere inside the Senate buildings, doing things in places they shouldn't be, excited by the fear of getting caught.

Every sound we made seemed to echo throughout the entire building as we entered Dan's office.

He switched on the fluorescent lights, and suddenly, it didn't seem like such a sexy idea anymore.

"Damn. The senator's door is locked," Dan said, trying the knob.

He pulled a credit card from his wallet.

"You're breaking and entering!" I said as he tried to card the lock.

The alcohol was wearing off and watching Dan try desperately to break into his senator's office wasn't exactly turning me on.

"Let's go," I said. "This is stupid."

"Then let's do it on my desk," Dan suggested.

I looked over at his cramped cubicle, and there was nothing sexy about it. He had a Me Wall with a large photo of himself standing next to Janet Reno.

"Are you serious?" I asked. "Let's just go back to my place."

"Oh, come on, Jackie. You know you want to," he said, backing me into the desk.

I rolled my eyes.

"No, I really don't," I said, pushing him off me, "and I'm a Taurus, so you can't make me change my mind."

He grabbed me by the waist and threw me over his desk.

"Dan! Stop it!" I shrieked, thrashing around beneath him. "Are you crazy?"

"Shhh," he warned. "You don't want this incident to end up on the front page of *Roll Call*, do you?"

I stopped struggling.

"That's a good girl," he said, unzipping his pants.

"I need to be drunk! I need lube!" I kept telling him.

"No you don't," he said. "Just relax."

I took a deep breath.

"But it's going to hurt," I said, squirming.

"I want it to hurt," he told me, spreading my ass cheeks apart. "I want you to feel every *vein*."

It was always interesting to give yourself over to a man and see what he would do with you, to see how far he would go, to find out just how nasty he really was. You learned a lot about a person this way. I would just watch guys do whatever freaky thing it was that got them off, and I would think to myself, *Whoa, this person is totally crazy.* And my next thought would be, *I can't wait to tell the girls all about it!*

On the way out of the building, one of the security guards asked us if we had a good time.

I asked the guard if he had ever caught anybody while they were doing it.

"Only once," he told us.

"Did you arrest them?" I asked.

"Oh, no," the guard replied. "I just said, 'Excuse me, Senator' and closed the door behind me."

I rolled my eyes at Dan as we exited the building.

"Do you believe that story?" I asked him as we walked back to my place. "Would a senator be stupid enough to do something like that?"

"What about us? Are we stupid?" Dan asked.

"Yeah, but we're not elected officials," I reminded him. "We could still lose our jobs if anyone found out about this."

"What about that security guard?" I asked. "What's stopping him from blackmailing us or something?"

"That guy isn't looking for trouble. He just wants to get his paycheck and go home at the end of the day."

"And you're counting on that?" I asked. "What if he's some evil genius?"

"Then he wouldn't be working as a security guard," Dan tittered.

"And he wouldn't be wasting his time trying to hustle a no-money bum like you," I said only half-joking. "He'd stick to catching congressmen with their pants down if he wanted to cash out of here."

"For your information, I'm looking for a job," Dan told me as we rounded the corner on Pennsylvania Avenue. "I can double or triple my salary on K Street."

"Really?" I asked. "You're leaving the Hill?"

"I've been here long enough," he replied. "It's time to start making big money in the private sector."

With these magic words, Dan suddenly became potential boyfriend material. If not, at least he would be gone soon. No more awkward moments running into him on the Senate campus.

# Chapter 15

The next morning, I spent another three hours with my friends on Instant Messenger, telling them all about my date in Dan's office last night. Meanwhile, the pile of unopened mail on my desk grew larger. I loved my friends, but this was getting out of control.

Then it dawned on me. The best way to keep my friends up-to-date was to start keeping a Web log on the Internet. I could post things gossip-item style, like Blogette did on her site. All I had to do was write an update every so often, and my friends could check in on my life whenever they felt like it. It was free, easy, and what a time-saver!

I set up my blog, amazed at how simple it was to self-publish on the Web. I could write anything I wanted to and nobody could stop me. I typed the words *April is a butt* into my template and clicked on the Post icon.

And there it was, on the World Wide Web. I e-mailed her the link, and a minute later, she called me on my cell phone, demanding that I take it down.

How fun. The possibilities were endless.

My friends set up blogs of their own, too. We surmised that our productivity at work would go up, and that might lead to promotions.

But we decided against password-protecting our blogs. The whole point of all of this was *convenience*. Passwords were just too much trouble. What interest would strangers have in our lives anyway? With millions of blogs on the Web, they would have to be pretty hard up to care about any of the dumb bullshit we were writing about. We chose only to keep them anonymous, using pseudonyms or initials, just in case.

First, my blog needed a name. I had always thought that *Washingtonian* magazine needed a fashion supplemental. (Washington women could not dress themselves for shit.) I had the perfect name for it, too: *Washingtonienne* magazine. Cute, right? But since they were too stupid to come up with that one on their own, I'd use the name for my blog instead.

Unfortunately, I didn't have time to post anything at first because the senator's wife was in the office all week. She came by every so often in her hideous St. John suits and David Yurman necklaces to make us rearrange the furniture in the front office, or reshelve all the books so that the bookcases looked "less busy." Never mind that we all had jobs that we were supposed to be doing.

Apparently, every senator's wife thought she was Jackie Kennedy, and that her husband's office was her own little White House. I suppose those were the perks of marrying well.

As I was pruning the plants in the front office at the behest of the senator's wife, my cell phone rang. It was my sister, Lee, asking if she could borrow some more money. I hoped she might have some news about Mom and Dad, but she was just as clueless as I was about the divorce.

I went over to the post office in the Dirksen Building to mail her another check. Of course, Dan would have to be there, too.

I wasn't really *mad* at him, but he wasn't my favorite person in the world, either. I greeted him cordially like a grown-up and took my place in line.

He dropped to the back of the line to stand next to me.

"Your ass looks great in that dress," he said in a low voice.

I rolled my eyes and sighed.

"Your ass looks great, too," I said loud enough for everyone to hear.

Dan's face turned red, and I couldn't help but laugh at him. Despite his arrogance, he embarrassed pretty easily.

I ended up going to lunch with him that day. It was the first of several appearances together in the cafeteria, and by the end of the week, we were an "item."

Random people in my office wanted to know if Dan was my boyfriend. Even Janet asked me, "Who is that guy you're always prancing around with in the cafeteria?"

*Prancing?* I guess I must have looked happy when I was with him. I suppose that I was, if only on a highly superficial level: He was the closest thing that I had to a boyfriend at the time. But the guy just didn't make my heart skip a beat.

Eventually, Dan would surely stop calling me, so I could just wait it out and avoid the awkwardness of ending it with him. In the meantime, I had someone to make out with, which was good enough for me.

WE WENT TO LAURA'S "going away" party at Kelly's Irish Times to celebrate her new job. Some dude she was fucking finally got her a job at his lobbying firm. I guess that sleeping your way to the top actually worked. I knew from experience that a blow job could get you a career as a letter opener in the United States Senate.

"Aren't you going to miss working on the Hill?" I asked her.

"It's bittersweet, you know? Like when you graduate from high school. You know you'll miss it, but at the same time, you can't wait to leave," she told me.

"How long have you been here?"

"A little over a year. But trust me, it feels *much* longer, like dog years. How long do you think you'll stay?"

"I want to make a career of it."

"Are you serious?" Laura asked. "I can't see you staying here much longer."

"I can write a fucking form letter," I said defensively. "I used to be a writer, you know."

"*Anyone* can write a form letter, Jackie. A retarded

monkey could be an LC. What I mean is that you'd be better off doing something else. You're just not the Hill type."

"What does that mean?" I asked. "I'm *here*, aren't I?"

"Yeah, but *look* at you."

I looked down at my leopard-print D&G dress and gold heels. I had put on a black cardigan to make my outfit look more conservative, which was a huge concession on my part: It was a shame to cover up such an expensive dress.

"Well, it's not like I'm down on the Senate floor or anything," I argued. "If there was a problem with the way I dress, I'm sure someone would have pulled me aside and mentioned it to me by now."

"Of course no one is actually going to *say* anything to you about it," Laura said. "They'll just talk about you behind your back. That's the way that people here operate."

"I thought you political types were supposed to be opinionated and outspoken. What a bunch of pussies."

April and Tom finally showed up, looking like the perfect Capitol Hill couple in his and hers navy suits from Brooks Brothers. They had just come from dinner at La Colline, paid for by the pro-life lobby. (Congressional staffers were famous dinner whores.)

"You're not pro-life, are you?" I asked April.

"No, but I'm pro free dinner," she said, rubbing her belly. "What's Laura drinking tonight? I need to buy her one at some point tonight."

"Don't bother," I told her. "She's already double-fisting Ketel One martinis. At this rate, I doubt she'll make it past Happy Hour."

April spotted Dan coming out of the men's room.

"Are you here with *him*?" she asked me. "I thought he wanted to keep it on the Q-T."

I shrugged.

"I don't know *what* we're doing," I admitted. "We're just having fun, I suppose."

"Why are you wasting your time with Dan?" April asked me. "Are you that desperate?"

"I could ask the same question of you," I replied, nodding toward Tom, who was tapping away furiously at his BlackBerry in the middle of the bar. "Are you sure you can't do better than *that*?"

It was a terrible thing to say because April actually cared about Tom in a way that my apathetic, immature mind couldn't comprehend.

She threw her drink on my sweater and walked out of the bar, dragging Tom behind her.

"What the fuck?" Laura wanted to know.

I took off my sweater and told her what happened.

"Don't go after them," she told me. "Let them feel superior all by themselves."

Laura was so much cooler than April. Why didn't I hang out with her more often?

We ended up getting trashed with Dan, who took us downstairs to the supercheesey dance floor.

Who knew that Irish bars had dance floors in their basements? Only in DC, I guess. I remember the deejay playing a lot of Nelly and Britney Spears. I also remember the three of us taking turns giving each other lap dances, and stuffing money down each other's pants. But I don't remember how the three of us ended up back at my new apartment.

. . .

I WOKE UP IN BED ALONE the next morning, naked except for my bra.

In college, this would be one of those innocent "oh my God, we were *sooo* fucked-up!" situations. Now it was just scary. My mind raced with questions:

*How did I get here?*

*What had they done to me?*

*Did anyone from work see me?*

*Were pictures taken?*

*Where is my wallet?*

*Where are they, and what are they doing now?*

I heard Laura giggling from the living room, and I got a bad feeling about what might have happened while I was passed out.

Assuming that the two of them might be fucking, I put my underpants back on and tiptoed down the hallway so I could catch them in the act.

Much to my surprise, they were both fully clothed.

"Good morning, Sleeping Beauty," Dan said, kissing me on the cheek.

"What happened last night?" I asked. "Did you guys fuck?"

They both told me that they hadn't. According to them, we had taken a cab from the Irish Times because I wanted to show them the apartment. Then we attempted to have a threesome, but I changed my mind and backed out.

"That doesn't sound like something I would do," I said.

"You were really out of it," Laura told me. "So we let you sleep in your bed, and we slept out here on the floor."

(I still hadn't bought any furniture for my new apartment.)

"And you guys didn't fuck?" I asked.

Again, they denied it.

"Okay," I said, "let's not make a *thing* out of this. If something happened, let's get it out into the open."

"I wish there was more to tell," Dan told me, "but really, nothing happened."

I looked at the boy who was supposed to be my boyfriend, and the girl who was supposed to be my new friend, and I realized that I really didn't know either of these people at all. How could I know if they were telling the truth? The most convenient thing for everyone involved was to go along with their story, especially since I wanted to believe that Dan and Laura actually gave a shit about me.

Dan made excuses to leave the apartment first, leaving Laura and me alone to see who would blink first.

"This is another one of those things that we should keep between us girls," she told me.

"Including April?" I asked. "Because I tell her everything."

Or at least I used to, before I let a fucker like Dan come between us because I let my crotch do all of my thinking for me.

"If you tell her, she'll say 'I told you so' and pretend that she's better than us just because she has a boyfriend—who she cheats on, by the way," Laura reminded me. "That girl doesn't know who she is anymore."

I was having one of those Carrie Bradshaw "I couldn't help but wonder" moments: *Did any of us really know who we were?*

After Laura left, I went to the fridge for a bottle of Fiji. And that's when I saw it.

Dan's bottle of Astroglide on my kitchen counter. With the cap off.

*Oh.*

I tore my bedroom apart searching for my cell phone. I found it between my sheets, but I hesitated before pressing the *Call* button.

I really did not want to have this conversation, and there was a good chance that she might get angry and hang up on me. But even so, it was my chance to do the right thing, and the sooner I could set things straight, the better.

"I owe you an apology," I said when April answered her phone, and told her the whole story.

"They had sex on your living room floor while you were unconscious?" she asked incredulously.

"You were right about him," I admitted. "You were right about everything. I guess I'm one of those people who has to learn everything the hard way."

"Aren't you furious?" she asked. "If Laura fucked Tom, I would murder the both of them, then I would shoot myself."

"Dan and I are nothing like you and Tom," I explained.

"But still! What a fucked-up thing to do! That just goes to show how jealous and selfish people really are."

"But we were about to have a *threesome:* Dan and Laura would have ended up fucking at some point anyway. Besides, this is exactly what I deserve for fucking your crush in the first place!"

"I guess you don't have any right to be mad then, do you?" April laughed.

"That's *exactly* how I feel! This is my punishment and I need to take it like a man. Only, if I were a man, I probably would have punched someone in the face by now."

"I just regret having any kind of affection for Dan whatsoever," April admitted. "He made total jackasses out of us, and he's not even all that great."

"You had sex with Dan?" I asked. "When did this happen?"

"I thought you knew," April said. "Dan and I were having an affair while Tom was in New Hampshire."

"Why didn't you tell me this before?"

"He wanted to keep it a secret, and now I know why: so he could make moves on other girls in the office behind my back."

"He was probably more afraid of getting his ass kicked by Tom."

"I was so ready to dump Tom for Dan, but then you came along. Naturally, I was jealous at first, especially when I saw you with Dan in the cafeteria looking so cute together. But now I realize that you stopped me from making a huge mistake."

"Uh, thanks."

"I know that Dan can be charming, so don't feel stupid. At least Laura was around to stop *you* from getting in too deep."

"So you're not mad at me?" I asked.

"Not anymore," April replied. "But can you believe all three of us have fucked the same guy? It's so incestuous."

"Yeah, I can't believe Laura would want our *leftovers*."

I was glad that April and I could joke about something that didn't seem so funny at first. It would make great material for my blog, I thought. I ran a bath for myself, contemplating how I would write it up when I sat down at my computer on Monday morning. Then my phone rang.

It was Laura with some unsurprising news.

"I have to tell you something," she began. "I think I might have had sex with Dan last night."

"What do you mean?" I asked. "You're not sure?"

"I was pretty drunk," she explained. "I don't remember much."

"So why didn't you bring this up earlier, when all three of us were in the same room?"

"I don't know, Jackie. I was embarrassed."

"Well, how does your ass feel today? Does it hurt? Because Dan's a pretty big guy, or didn't you notice?"

"Don't be gross. This is difficult enough as it is."

"You're not telling me this just to hurt me, are you?"

"Of course not. That's the last thing I want to do."

"Then tell me what happened, Laura. Bring it on. I can take it."

She took a deep breath and admitted that yes, Dan had fucked her on my living room floor while I was passed out in the other room.

"Are you mad at me?" she asked.

"I'm just glad that you finally told me the truth," I told her. "You're my friend, Laura. I'm not going to throw you away over this bullshit."

"Don't you care? I mean, I thought you really liked Dan."

"Not so much," I said dismissively. "I can always get another boyfriend."

"So you're breaking up with him?"

"I don't know. I suppose I'll talk it over with him when he comes over tomorrow night."

"You're going to have sex with him?" Laura asked incredulously.

"Yeah, I probably will," I admitted. "So what?"

"Then there's something else I have to tell you."

"Now what?"

"I have HPV."

"HPV?" I asked. "What the fuck is that?"

"Human papillomavirus."

"You mean genital warts?"

"It's the virus that *causes* genital warts, actually."

"Is that better?"

"A lot of people in DC have them. It's like an epidemic."

"Who told you that?" I asked. "I've never heard anything about it."

"My gynecologist," Laura replied. "When he told me, he said that he had, like, thirty other women he had to call with the same thing."

"A genital warts epidemic? What is this, the seventies?"

"I'm telling you this because I don't want you to catch it from Dan," Laura told me. "We didn't use any protection last night. You have to promise that you won't have sex with him!"

"Ew, don't worry," I replied. "But you have to tell Dan ASAP. You don't want him spreading genital warts all over the Hill, do you?"

"Maybe I do!" she laughed. "After all, everything that goes around, comes around."

Just when I thought the nightlife in DC couldn't get any worse, an HPV epidemic breaks out. I sank into my bathtub after I got off the phone with Laura, realizing that I had just been fucked over by the people who called themselves my friends.

I guess April was right: We were all jealous and selfish people, especially at our age. We treated each other like shit, but as long as we did so with smiles on our faces, we all remained friends.

Why did everything have to be *political*? Maybe I was socializing with the wrong people.

LATER THAT DAY, I GOT another surprise phone call. Sean the bike messenger wanted to "hang out," so I invited him over to see my new apartment.

He rode his bike all the way from Adams Morgan to Capitol Hill, so his body gave off a ripe smell that was kind of sexy, but I imagined that his balls probably stank. No way was I ever giving him a blow job.

I let him into the apartment, and he pulled out a nice selection of drugs from his messenger bag.

"Do I have to pay?" I asked.

"That all depends on you," he answered, leaning in to kiss me.

He had a hard-on, which I could *smell* at this point. It sickened me to think that I had snorted lines off it a few weeks ago. The things we did for drugs!

The odor nauseated me when he pulled it out of his shorts, and I immediately turned my head away in response.

It was really too bad.

"I don't feel good," I told him. "Can we just lie down?"

He shrugged, tucking his boner back into his shorts. He looked kind of pissed.

"Where's the TV?" he asked.

"I don't have one," I told him. "I don't spend much time at home."

"Can we go to my house?" he whined. "I have a DVD player and everything."

"Okay, but we're taking a cab."

I wasn't about to ride all the way up to Adams Morgan on his handlebars.

Back at his place, I did a few lines (off the coffee table) and agreed to let him fuck me as long as he took a shower first.

We stayed up all night, snorting coke, fucking, and watching *Fight Club* over and over again on DVD.

Sean had all these cool stories about beating up Skinheads and going to "juvie" when he was a kid growing up in Philly.

"Check out this scar," he said, turning around. "Some dude stabbed me in the back when I was twelve."

Damn, he was sexy. We didn't have guys like this on the Hill.

"You're a fun girl," he said as the sun came up. "We should hang out all the time. I'm totally serious."

"Totally!" I agreed. "Oh my God, you know what we should do today? We should do Robo! And walk around taking pictures of stuff!"

"That would be awesome, but I can't today. I have stuff I need to do."

Huh? For a few seconds there, I thought Sean actually liked me, but now he was giving me the same line that I had given Dan.

When Sean went to the bathroom that morning, I swiped half of his stash. I just couldn't leave a relationship empty-handed.

# Chapter 16

I met April at Murky Coffee, back in Capitol Hill. I looked like such an obvious druggie, wearing oversized sunglasses, sniffing incessantly, and nursing a triple-shot skim latte to fight off the inevitable coke headache.

"Jackie, you're my hero," April said, "but you should take a night off every once in a while. You're not a party animal anymore."

"I'm not?" I asked. "But I'm still in my twenties. This is what I'm *supposed* to be doing on the weekends."

"Yeah, but eventually, you'll have to move on from this. You don't want to be fucking a bike messenger when you're thirty."

"*Thirty?* But thirty is still young! More like forty."

"Jackie, by then you'll probably be dead."

I rolled my eyes behind my dark glasses.

"What are we doing today?" I asked. "I'm sick of sitting here."

April looked up from the front page of the Sunday *New York Times* she was reading.

"Why don't you go home and get some rest," she suggested.

"I can't sleep," I replied, "and I can't think of anything else to do besides shopping."

"We live in *Washington, DC,*" April reminded me. "Wouldn't you rather go to a museum or something?"

"Too many tourists. Besides, I've already seen all that junk."

"But all you ever do is shop. It's such an empty pastime."

"Well, duh, I'm shallow. Look," I said, holding up the "SundayStyles" section of the *Times.* "This is the first and only section I read, and I don't even read it, I just look at the pictures. April, won't you please go shopping with me?"

WE TOOK A CAB TO Georgetown because April wanted to go to the H&M there. As we teetered down the brick sidewalks of M Street in our high heels, I made a mental note to myself never to move to Georgetown. It was damn near impossible to walk in heels there.

"Ooh!" I shrieked. "We *have* to go in here. I need a new Katie!"

The gorgeous Kate Spade shopgirls (and shopguy) greeted us as I dragged April into the boutique. All of the most fabulous people in DC worked in retail. Unlike the nerds running the country from Capitol Hill, *they* knew something about public service.

"I can't afford this store," April protested as she examined a pink leather handbag. "Let's go to H&M."

I looked at the price tag.

"Two hundred dollars? That one is probably on sale," I told her. "Have you ever been to Chanel? The bags there are, like, two thousand, at least."

She rolled her eyes at me.

"I'm perfectly happy with the Coach bag I have now," she sniffed.

April didn't know that her bag was made in China rather than Italy but cost the same as the Katie she was looking at now. But then again, April *wouldn't* have known. She knew nothing about this sort of stuff, except for what I told her. (She never did any postgrad time in New York.)

I didn't want to get into a pissing match with her over handbags, so I didn't say anything. Instead, I tried on a pair of three-hundred-dollar earrings that looked fabulous on me.

"I can't believe you would spend that kind of money on a pair of earrings," April grumbled.

"Three hundred dollars is cheap for jewelry," I said defensively. "If a man only spent three hundred dollars on jewelry for me, I'd dump his ass."

I whipped out my envelope and bought the earrings with the cash inside.

"Did Fred give you that?" April asked, obviously upset by my gauche spending. "Where do you plan on wearing those things? You can't wear them to the office or you'll look ridiculous."

"Spending money just feels good," I explained. "It's such a *release*—it's better than sex."

"I can't believe this," April said, stopping in the middle of the sidewalk on the way to H&M. "I can barely pay my rent, and you're dropping cash all over the place just because it *feels good*? Do you really think that's fair?"

"Nothing in life is fair, April. Working on the Hill for twenty-five thousand dollars a year was your choice. But you're a young, pretty girl living in a town full of shallow, horny men. If you're not making the most of an unfair advantage, well, that's your own stupid fault."

April scowled at me.

"And I suppose that you're the smart one, getting dumped by your fiancé?" she asked. "Now you're making twenty-five thousand on the Hill, dating assholes who treat you like a whore. That's not smart, Jackie, that's pathetic!"

I shook my head in disagreement.

"No, I *was* pathetic," I argued. "I hated myself for giving up my independence because I wanted Mike to take care of me. But I've found a way to keep my independence and still get what I want from other people. *That's* what makes me the smart one."

"I still think you're pathetic," April said as we entered the store. "But from now on, you're buying all of my drinks."

# Chapter 17

Do you ever feel like you're not accomplishing anything at all? That's what working on the Hill was like. Maybe somebody somewhere was working hard, but I only knew what I saw: lots of people with way too much free time on their hands.

Dan called my cell a few times before he resorted to calling me out over Instant Messenger Monday afternoon. He knew I was at my desk because his Buddy List showed that I was "Available."

I wrote back telling him that I couldn't talk because I was about to get lunch, and who do I see in the cafeteria five minutes later?

Dan must have run down there as soon as we signed off.

"What a coincidence," he said as he followed me to the checkout.

"Yeah, it's uncanny," I said as Dan paid for my Diet Dr Pepper.

"Let's sit over here," he suggested, setting his tray down on one of the high-visibility tables right next to the checkout.

"I'm going back upstairs, actually," I told him. "I have stuff to do today."

"I guess the mail isn't going to sort itself," he said, patting me on the ass.

I looked at him, astonished that he would do such a thing in the middle of the Senate cafeteria. He smiled, daring me to make a scene here. Well, he asked for it.

"You left your Astroglide at my apartment on Saturday!" I said loudly.

He dragged me out of the dining room.

"Jackie, what is your problem?" he asked. "Why are you hell-bent on embarrassing me?"

"Do you *always* carry a bottle of lube around with you wherever you go?" I asked, ignoring his question.

"Of course not!"

"Oh, that's right, I almost forgot. *Every vein.*"

Dan's face turned red.

"Jackie, please, not here," he begged. "We'll talk later, okay?"

"We don't need to talk about this," I told him. "I think you should just stop calling me."

"Where is this coming from? Do you think I did something with Laura because there was lube on your kitchen counter?"

I rolled my eyes.

"I know what happened," I informed him. "She told me everything."

"Did she?" Dan asked. "Because I think you should know that your friend is a little unstable. She was acting very strangely that night."

"Why would Laura lie about something like this? Are you trying to create reasonable doubt?"

"Well, it's my word against hers."

"Yeah, and everyone is a liar, so I don't know who to believe. It's like something out of *Cruel Intentions*, and I'm sick of all this intrigue, Dan. Just tell me what happened."

Again, I gave him a chance to tell the truth and he blew it. Nevertheless, part of me wanted to believe that he was a faithful partner to me, and I began to doubt Laura's confession, suspecting that maybe she made it all up so she could have Dan to herself.

I didn't know what to think anymore. I was on my way to meet Fred that afternoon, so I had no right to be mad at Dan anyway.


MEETING AT MY apartment wasn't as sexy as the hotel, but since Fred was paying the rent, I couldn't really complain.

Right or wrong, the "married-man-and-his-young-mistress" thing made for some of the hottest sex of my life. He fucked like a prisoner out on parole, admiring my soft skin and slender body. He asked me to keep getting waxed, and I wanted to give him his money's worth so I obliged him.

"My little girl," he would say over and over again as he

fucked me. If he was taking too long to finish, all I had to do was say something like, "Oh, Daddy, please, harder!" and that was all it took. He loved that.

Most older guys do. They get off on that father figure stuff. But sometimes Fred took a condescending tone toward me that really pissed me off. He was always lecturing me about stuff and counting the number of times that I'd say the word *like* in a sentence.

"It makes you sound unintelligent," he told me.

"That's how people my age talk," I explained. "If you don't like it, then maybe you should have an affair with a woman your own age."

"Well, it's a lazy way of talking," he replied. "People your age need to realize that it's not cool to be lazy."

Like, since when? The guy was paying my rent and giving me an allowance for doing absolutely nothing.

Older men loved people my age when they were getting off on our hot young bodies. But then they'd always be so disappointed when they realized that we were so *immature.*

Like, duh, of course I was immature: I was half his age! That was why he was fucking me instead of his wife, remember?

But, like I said, the sex was great. Despite whatever else was going on in our lives, Fred and I could always meet up somewhere for a few hours and make each other happy. It was as if our relationship existed in a vacuum: It would begin at noon and end about an hour later, confined within my bedroom walls. Then we'd go back to our real lives as if nothing had happened. It was total sexcapism. But unfortunately, my long lunches were starting to arouse suspicion among my coworkers. I always told them that I had doctors' appointments, and they probably wondered what sort of crazy problems I had that I needed to see a doctor three times a week.

But I wasn't seeing any doctor (although maybe I should have been), because I felt fabulous. Maybe I should have felt bad about carrying on an affair with a married man, but the bad feelings just weren't there. If he didn't feel bad about it, then why should I?

But we had a problem.

"I think my wife knows," Fred told me one day.

This was *after* we had sex, of course.

"How *much* does she know?" I asked him. "Like, does she know my name?"

"She knows your name, she knows where you work, your phone number, your address."

Obviously, Fred had fucked up.

"She was looking through my BlackBerry in the car while I was driving," he explained. "She saw your name in there and asked me who you were."

"You didn't tell her about *this*, did you?"

I hoped that Fred the chief of staff was a smarter man than that, if not for my own sake, then for the sake of the federal government.

"I told her that you were the contact person in your office," he explained, "but she might call to check, so don't answer your phone for a few days."

I let out a sigh of relief. Compared to what could have happened, missing a few phone calls was no problem.

"Poor Fred," I said, rubbing his shoulders. "You must be worried sick over this."

"Forget about it," he said. "I already have."

I kept rubbing even though I was supposed to be back at my desk about twenty minutes ago.

"You're so good to me, Jacqueline," he said. "Sometimes I spend all day thinking about running away with you. I would never actually do it, but I think about it all the time. If I ever asked you to run away with me, would you?"

*Fuck.*

This was not supposed to happen. We had an arrangement: He used me for sex, and I used him for money. I thought it was pretty straightforward.

I had never stopped to think about how I really felt about Fred, because I wouldn't let myself have feelings for a married man with a baby.

Why get my hopes up? And what would I be hoping for anyway? That Fred would dump his wife? That his baby would grow up without a father? Even *I* knew that was just plain wrong.

Meanwhile, Fred had been sitting in his office all this time, daydreaming about doing these things, and now he was asking if I'd go along with it.

"You shouldn't say things like that," I told him. "You might just get what you wish for."

When I got back to the office, there was a voice mail from Laura, inviting me out to dinner at the Palm, another favorite restaurant of the expense account crowd.

"Let's drink martinis and order steaks," I suggested, "like a couple of real fat cats."

"So long as we talk politics for a few minutes, I can expense everything because you're a Senate employee," Laura explained. "No one has to know that you're Staff Ass."

*Chapter 18*

Laura wore a bright red Chanel suit, a gift she had bought herself with her signing bonus. I wore a gray Calvin Klein shift dress, a gift I had bought myself with Fred's cash.

It was classic. We spotted George Stephanopoulos *and* James Carville in the restaurant before our martinis had even arrived.

"How sad is that?" Laura mused. "Those are the biggest celebrities Washington has to offer, and they're not even attractive."

"I don't see any hotties here at all," I observed, spinning my head to get a look around. "Hollywood for the Ugly."

"Except for us, of course," Laura said as we clinked glasses.

We were pretty trashed by the time our steaks arrived. We barely touched them as they cooled off on our plates. Ordering steaks seemed like the right thing to do at the time, despite having no appetite because of the blow we did in the bathroom when we arrived.

That was the thing we girls loved about coke. It gave you such a nice, skinny feeling.

"Do you think we'll ever have our pictures on the wall here?" Laura asked, gazing at the caricature of James Carville's dog.

"We'd have to get famous somehow," I reminded her, "and you can't really get famous working on the Hill."

"No, I suppose you can't. Not unless you do something really bad."

"Who wants to be famous anyway? I'd rather just get rich."

"Well, you can't get rich working on the Hill, either. You'll have to marry someone with money. Either that, or go back to school."

"I'd like to go back to school, but I still don't know what I want to be when I grow up."

"You should really be a writer, Jackie."

"I tried that once, but it didn't work out. Where is our waiter?" I asked, changing the subject.

"We should order champagne," Laura suggested, looking around. "Jackie, I think that guy over there is checking you out!"

"What guy?" I asked, turning around.

"The guy in the suit who looks like an asshole. The older one."

I turned again. Yes, he looked like an asshole, and yes, he was looking at me. It seemed like assholes were always looking at me.

"Why do I keep getting the old ones?" I asked.

"I think it's your face," Laura said thoughtfully.

"My face?"

"You have a classic face."

"What the fuck does that mean? Do I look old?"

"No, I mean you have a *classic face*. It's pretty."

"Are you saying that young guys don't like pretty faces?"

"No, I don't think that they do anymore. They're more into the body these days."

"What is that supposed to mean? That I don't have a good body? Laura, by now I'm used to the fact that every guy likes you better than me. You don't need to insult my body to prove that point."

I imagined Dan comparing my body to Laura's, and the thought was absolutely nauseating.

"Your body is fine," Laura reassured me. "You're just a little too thin, that's all."

She knew exactly the right thing to say. To us, "too thin" was the ultimate compliment.

"Did you ever get around to calling Dan?" I asked. "I saw him in the cafeteria today, and he didn't say anything to me about *you know what*."

"No, but he called my office today," Laura told me. "We're going out to dinner tomorrow, so I'll probably tell him about *you know what* afterwards."

"You guys are *dating* now?" I asked incredulously. "How did this happen?"

"He said that he wanted to hear all about my new job, and he asked me out for a drink. Then I suggested that we get dinner instead. It's not really a *date* per se."

"But you obviously like him if you're inviting him out to dinner."

"Well, it's not as if you and Dan are *serious*. You're always saying how much you hate guys who work on the Hill."

I suppose that she was right. Obviously, Dan and I weren't serious if he was calling Laura's office and asking her out for drinks, so why should I care?

Sure, they had already fucked, but I thought that was just incidental to *my* sexy relationship with Dan. I guess if they liked each other, I should have been happy for them, but I couldn't help but feel slighted. At least I knew where things stood with us.

"If you like Dan, then you owe it to yourself to pursue a relationship with him," I told Laura. "But he rims me, you know."

Laura winced at this.

"God, Jackie, you're so vulgar!" she groaned.

"Well, it's a vulgar age," I replied.

"That guy keeps looking over here," Laura whispered to me, changing the subject. "Maybe you should go talk to him."

"What am I supposed to do? Go over there and offer him a table dance? Besides, I don't hit on guys. They hit on *me*. But, look, I'll give him some eye contact, and he'll come over in no time."

Instead, the waiter walked over to our table with a message.

"The gentleman seated in the corner would like to pay your bill this evening," he informed us.

Laura nodded her approval. Like me, she saw nothing wrong with leaving the Palm with a total stranger.

No matter how many expensive meals we ate here, or how much our designer outfits cost, girls like us would never be fat cats. In this town, we were nothing but pussy.

HE TOLD ME THAT HIS name was Paul as we got into the cab. He was a fund-raiser for the Democrats and was in town from Boston.

"Where to?" the driver asked.

"The Hay-Adams," Paul answered.

He explained to me that he needed to stop by his room to check for a very important fax that he was expecting. I knew this was bullshit, but since I had nothing else to do that night, why not get to know somebody new?

His eyes ran over my body as I sat next to him in the cab, assuring himself that he had chosen wisely from the selection of available women at the Palm. He probably went there whenever he was in town, waiting for some girl like me with a "classic face," who had no boyfriend to take her out. Some girl who worked on the Hill and made shit money at her job, who would jump at the chance of fucking a Very Important Person such as himself.

He told me that I was the prettiest girl at the Palm, which I guess was supposed to be a compliment. Then he asked the driver to stop and wait at the CVS in Dupont Circle.

"I have to get something," was all he said, but I already knew that he was going in to buy condoms.

He tried to hide them from me when he got back into the car, holding the translucent plastic bag behind his back. He offered me gum as a distraction, but I could see through the bag that he had also purchased Magnums.

*Well, at least he's big,* I thought.

We went up to Paul's room, where he checked the fax machine for that important thingy he was waiting for. Of course, it hadn't arrived yet, but it should at any minute, and would I mind waiting a few minutes for it to arrive? It was *really* important.

He told me that I could watch some television if I wanted, so I took the remote and reclined on the bed, flipping channels.

"What's on?" he asked, sitting down on the bed next to me.

But he wasn't looking at the television screen. He was looking down at me, with his hand hovering over my body, waiting for just the right moment to make his move.

I looked him in the eye and unbuttoned my shirt so he could see underneath.

He took my hand and placed it on his crotch so that I understood what we would be doing tonight, but I had known the moment I got into the cab with him that we were going to fuck.

Paul was one of those Jekyll-and-Hyde types who seemed like your average horny dude, but as soon as you got in bed with him, watch out! He started fucking me without putting on one of those condoms he'd stopped to buy, and he actually put his hand over my mouth so that I couldn't object. He pulled out instead, shooting his load all over my chest.

"Whose office do you work for?" he asked me as we disengaged.

I answered him, wiping the ejaculate off my chest with a tissue. I threw it on the floor with attitude, fighting the urge to throw it in his face.

"Do they know what a slut you are?" he asked, stroking himself.

Paul was obviously a sicko who got off on making me feel uncomfortable, but his question confounded me. Could I possibly get fired for being a slut? Was my behavior "improper conduct reflecting upon the Senate office," or was it no one's business but my own?

Whenever April and I went to Capitol Lounge or one of the other bars on the Hill, we'd see congressional staffers hooking up and going home with strangers all the time, so I knew I wasn't the only one slutting around: It was common practice, and I wasn't doing anything illegal, so as an American woman, didn't I have the *right* to be a slut?

In New York, young professionals were encouraged to have sexy, exciting personal lives. If you could get clients into the hot club of the moment, or if you were sleeping with the CEO of a Fortune 500 company, you were seen as a valuable asset to any organization. But in Washington, people looked down on us girls who wanted to live the Fly Life. Maybe it was something of a character flaw, but what else were we supposed to do? Spend our evenings reading briefs? There was plenty of time for that once we got old and guys stopped asking us out. Even if I was ending up in hotel rooms with freaky perverts like Paul, at least it got me out of the house.

"Are we going to fuck again or what?" I asked him impatiently. "I don't have time for these mind games."

So we did, and afterward, Paul ordered room service and invited me up to Boston for the weekend.

"Maybe when the weather gets warmer," I lied. "Boston's too cold for me."

The truth was that this was a one-night stand if there ever was one.

"You should come up for the convention in July," he suggested. "I think we'd have a lot of fun."

"Yeah, call me. You know where I work," I reminded him. "But do me a favor?"

"Sure. What is it?"

"Please don't tell anybody what a slut I am."


BACK AT THE OFFICE, I often found myself rereading the same letter, like, six times before I could discern what the person was writing about. My eyes would just glaze over whenever I started to read. I wondered if I had undiagnosed ADD or something, but the truth was, I was just an apathetic brat who shouldn't have been working there.

But if I just sat at my desk, looking busy (which was easy to do with computers in the workplace), I would never get fired as long as I kept coming in. After all, "80 percent of success is showing up," and the other 20 percent is keeping up appearances.

My friends in New York said that blogging reminded them of the Web site that we worked on during the dot-com era. For me, it was a job in itself.

If you ask any blogger, they'll tell you that it quickly becomes an addiction. It was better than shopping and better than sex, because it was easy and free. (Sex is hard work if you're doing it right, and no, it ain't free. I'm *not* talking about prostitution. Just ask your boyfriend how much he's spent on drinks and dinners since you started dating. And how much have you spent on beauty treatments so that you'll look pretty for him? Sex is expensive, isn't it?)

Writing a blog gave me the opportunity to explain what was happening in my life on my own terms, to my friends, but more importantly, to myself. I was having trouble figuring it out.

Later, I would delete the whole thing and start all over again. It was like seeing a bad photo of yourself: The first thing you wanted to do was tear it up, but at some point, you had to accept that, yes, that's what you really looked like.

So enough with the self-loathing: I had nothing to be ashamed of, really. I was a bitchy slut and so were all of my friends. Why not put it out there? This was just between us girls anyway.

# Chapter 19

It started off innocently enough. April forwarded the link to four other people on the Hill.

Laura sent it to a few of her sorority sisters.

Diane forwarded it to her boyfriend.

Naomi sent it to a coworker.

And so on, and so on.

I was sort of flattered that my friends felt compelled to share my blog with others. It was as if I had my own little cult following. And when they would send me Instant Messages, pestering me to write more posts, I realized that I was giving them something to look forward to, just as I looked forward to reading Blogette every day.

But my friends' blogs were just as entertaining as mine, if not more so.

Naomi's was about how she had just broken up with her boyfriend and what it was like to be single again. (My favorite, because I could relate.)

Diane's was mostly about how much she hated her co-workers at *Brides* magazine (a Condé Nast publication).

Laura's was mostly about her new job and Dan's strange sexual antics.

But nothing could top April's M&Ms story. The New York girls were fascinated by our encounters with all of the closet freaks we met in Washington.

"I thought people in DC were supposed to be more dignified," Naomi told me over the phone.

"In Washington, you don't know what you're getting until it's too late," I explained. "Like, you think you've met this nice, normal guy, and then it turns out that he's into knife play or something."

"It's like living in a town full of Patrick Batemans."

"So do you still want to come visit me here?"

"Not really. But I think a weekend in the City would do you some good. Diane knows the deejay at that new club I was telling you about, so we're going on Saturday."

"*Everyone* says that they 'know the deejay.' We'd better not have to stand on line."

"Oh, we won't. But you should come up here for the weekend! I need another single girl to go out with. My married friends always have to go home early."

"I'll be there," I promised. "The two of us can stay out all night and do whatever we want."

I looked forward to going back to New York, but in the meantime, I had nothing left to do but *work*.

Janet sent me an e-mail reminder that my performance review was coming up next week, so I had to get rid of the weeks of backlogged mail that covered my desk before I left the office on Friday.

I tried drinking more coffee to boost my energy, but it only made me pee more. I needed something else.

I still had some of Sean's coke at home, so I tried doing some before I went to the office the next day, and the work just flew off of my desk! The days went by so much faster when I did a line or two. The cranky constituent letters no longer got me down. I was able to say, "People are crazy, God bless 'em!" and move on to the next pile without hesitation. I was no longer taking part in a conspiracy to dupe Middle America. I was keeping the dream alive!

I ran out of blow by Thursday, which gave me an excuse to ring up Sean. He didn't pick up when I called, so I assumed he was out on his bike.

About twenty minutes later, my phone rang.

"Is this Jacqueline Turner?" a girl's voice asked me when I picked up.

"Um, who is *this*?" I wanted to know.

"This is Sean's girlfriend."

How did this bitch get my number? Obviously, Sean had fucked up.

"Do you have black hair?" she asked. "Is it long?"

Why was she asking me about my *hair*, of all things?

"What is this about?" I asked.

"I think you know very well why I'm calling," she replied. "Apparently, you're fucking my boyfriend."

I didn't want to say anything to incriminate myself, nor

did I want to snitch on Sean. I had to be very careful, so as not to confirm or contradict whatever she thought had happened between me and her boyfriend.

"I'm sorry," I said, "but I think you might be confused."

"Oh, don't even try it! Sean already told me everything," she said.

I wondered what story he had told this girl. Did he tell her the truth, or did he lie, as I would have done?

"Does it make you feel good to fuck other people's boyfriends?" she asked. "You know, you shouldn't sleep with people you don't know very well. I'm telling you this for your own good."

Then I heard her say to someone, "What's wrong with her? She's not saying anything."

Most likely, it was Sean, shitting himself over what I might tell his girlfriend. I suppose this was her way of punishing him.

"I'm still here," I told her.

"Good. Because I want you to know that Sean and I have a very special relationship, and you're not going to ruin it for us. Hopefully, you'll find someone of your own who will love you as much as Sean loves me."

This girl was hysterical. I wanted to put her on speakerphone to give my officemates a good laugh, but decided that it wouldn't have been professional.

"And another thing, Jacqueline Turner. I know your name, I know your phone number, I know where you work, and I know where you live," she warned. "So don't fuck with me."

Then she hung up.

*Whoa.*

I wondered if she might actually come *here*, to the senator's office, to kick my ass. She sure sounded as if she were crazy enough to try it. And why did she ask about my hair? Did she know what I looked like? Was she watching me right now?

These careless flings were starting to cause a lot of stress in my life. Couldn't I just have a normal relationship with someone? How did I end up with all of these nonboyfriends anyway? Now was a good time to get out of town.

# Chapter 20

I love New York.

Why did I ever leave?

"Isn't that dress from, like, Fall '02?" Diane asked me, knowing very well that it was. "You're slipping, Jacqueline."

"I live in Washington now," I reminded them. "You have to pay retail for everything there."

"How do people live?" Naomi wondered, chewing her nicotine gum.

"But at least you can still smoke in DC."

"Really? Maybe I'll come visit you after all."

"You should take the Chinatown bus. It's only fifteen dollars."

"Really? They don't make you carry a chicken in your lap or anything, do they?"

I shook my head no.

"Then maybe I *will* take the bus to Washington. I'll check my calendar."

We wobbled over the cobblestones in the meatpacking district in our high heels, over to the club on Little West 12th Street. It was incredible that I had no problem getting in on a Saturday night in New York, but if I wanted to go to Saki on a Wednesday in DC, I had to stand on line. Life was always so unfair.

We scrambled down the narrow hallway to the pool-blue dance floor.

"Where's Kool-Aid?" Naomi asked some random model-actor who was drinking bottled water. (Only people on drugs would drink bottled water at a club.)

He pointed at a guy in a white Sean John hat, leaning against the wall near the restrooms.

"We didn't recognize you in the hat!" I told him.

Kool-Aid had been our dealer since college, when he used to work the big clubs like Twilo and Limelight. When City Hall decided to clean up the nightlife in New York, the dealers had to set up "boutiques" in the smaller clubs.

The procedure was as follows:

Stop and say hi to Kool-Aid on your way to the ladies' room. (That was when you told him how many pills you wanted.)

Go to the ladies' room, freshen up or whatever, then come back out and meet Kool-Aid at the bar.

Buy a drink or something and act like you're changing money with him. That's when the deal was made, and it looked totally legit. That was how Kool-Aid stayed out of the slammer all of these years. Smart guy.

"Long time, no see!" he said, kissing me on the cheek. "Where have you been, baby?"

"I moved to DC," I told him. "Before that, I was living with my boyfriend."

"Why would you do a stupid thing like that?"

"Which one?"

"Both!"

The guy had a point.

"I'll see you in *three* minutes," I told him. (Wink, wink.)

The ladies' room was full of Brazilian model-types, reapplying NARS Lip Lacquer and tossing their hair around. Naomi and I looked like trolls standing next to them.

"They don't have girls like these in Washington," I told Naomi. "Thank God!"

"After we get the drugs, let's go somewhere else," Naomi suggested.

"Oh, please! We can have anyone we want here. Guys love sluts!"

We left the bathroom and met Diane at the bar.

"Here, you guys," she said, slipping pills into our hands. "Take your brain medicine."

We all took turns dropping so we would come up at the same time.

"Jacqueline," Naomi said, gesturing toward a banquette on the opposite side of the room. "Isn't that Mike over there?"

We all turned to look.

It was him, with a perfect-looking blonde in a black Gucci cocktail dress. Drinking champagne, no less.

I blinked as tears rolled down my expressionless face. My friends looked very uncomfortable, not knowing what to do about me.

I wasn't *crying*, was I? Because this was really nothing to cry about. I already knew that Mike didn't love me anymore.

But to *see* it? *Ouch.*

Naomi took me aside, blotting my face with a cocktail napkin.

"Stop it, Jackie," she said. "*Stop caring.* If you don't cheer up right now, the E is going to make you cry all night long. *Stop caring!*"

"Let's get out of here," Diane suggested. "Let's go to Tribe."

"Tribe is on the other side of town!" Naomi argued. "I don't want to come up in a cab!"

"Well, we can't stay *here*."

"Jackie, where do *you* want to go?"

"I want to go back to Washington," I told them.

"Right now?" Naomi asked.

"I don't want to be here anymore."

"We can go someplace else, Jackie," Diane said, but she could tell by the stubborn look in my eye that I had already made up my mind. (I was a classic Taurus.)

# Chapter 21

I took the Acela back to Washington, instead of the Chinatown bus. I came up inside Penn Station, just as I was purchasing my tickets from one of those machines.

"I'm so much happier when I'm high," I sighed, not caring if anyone heard me.

Not caring. It felt so good.

Washington was really my favorite city anyway. It was the prettiest place I had ever lived, with fountains and flowering trees everywhere. And the rent here was far less expensive than Manhattan. I could see spending the rest of my life here: I'd get some fluffy government job, a couple of dogs, and live happily ever after.

And maybe—if I ever met someone in DC who I could

tolerate for more than a few hours—I would marry and have a baby someday.

But in the meantime, I could hardly take care of *myself*. I still hadn't bought any furniture for the apartment, and I didn't even know where the grocery store was in my neighborhood. (Whenever Fred came by, he would look at my bare rooms and empty refrigerator, and ask if I was "taking drugs.")

I wasn't even sure that I could hold down a job. I had one of the easiest jobs on the Hill, and I had a problem doing my work. Some days, I didn't do any work at all.

I had been dreading my work performance review all week. If I wasn't getting fired this time around, I would at least get a warning, accompanied by some humiliating lecture. I wasn't sure which was worse.

My drug-induced peak in productivity had backfired on me. While my output had increased, so did my margin of error. Constituents were calling the office complaining that their names had been misspelled on the response letters they received, or that they had received a letter about a different issue than the one they had written in about.

And since I was no longer high on the job, my productivity had gone way down.

My long lunches, constant tardiness, excessive personal calls, dress code violations, puking in the office bathroom, and erratic behavior in general made me more of a distraction than an asset to my office. And that was just the stuff they knew about!

But my review came back overwhelmingly positive: I was a "Very Good" employee.

Apparently, nobody knew what my job was, or what I was even doing in their office.

I went back to the Locker Room to watch back-to-back episodes of *Law & Order* at my desk, as I often did when I didn't have a lunch date with Fred.

Meghan, one of the senator's personal assistants, stopped by the Locker Room to microwave one of her disgusting Lean Cuisine frozen dinners.

I hardly ever spoke to her, so I was somewhat caught off-guard when she told me that my "boyfriend" (Dan) was in the cafeteria having lunch with another girl.

"I just think you should know," she said. "Janet says she saw them *talking*."

Talking? I wanted to tell Meghan that she and Janet should mind their own business, but I was also curious to see who Dan was "talking" to these days; if he wasn't "talking" to me or Laura, he was making fools of us by "talking" to other girls in the cafeteria.

I went down there and saw him sitting at his favorite table with a pretty girl wearing a purple-striped intern badge around her neck.

I didn't object when Laura told me about her dinner date with Dan just for this reason: I knew that he would fuck her over the way she had fucked me.

Like I said before, do you ever feel like you're not accomplishing anything at all?

AFTER WORK, I WALKED back to my apartment and threw myself on the bed. What did I have to look forward to? Really,

I needed to know. I needed a reason to get out of this bed tomorrow. My job was bullshit, my friends were totally shady, my love life was a disaster, and my own parents wouldn't return my phone calls.

Then I realized that the only thing I had to look forward to would be my next orgasm. Yes, sex was a free gift from God, wasn't it? I could always look forward to that.

So when Sean called me around midnight to apologize for his crazy girlfriend, I forgave him. His story was that his girlfriend had found several strands of my long, black hair in his bed. She threatened to call his probation officer (!) if he didn't tell her everything. And since she was such an obviously insecure psycho, she insisted on knowing *everything* about me so she could harass/scare/stalk me.

"The next time she catches you cheating, deny, deny, deny. To your very last breath," I advised him. "Now get on that bicycle of yours and pedal your ass down here ASAP. Oh, and bring your drugs."

I was tempted to call the police and tell them to put out an APB for a bike-riding drug dealer headed toward Capitol Hill. But then I wouldn't get the sex and drugs I needed to lift my spirits. I decided to wait until he left my apartment tomorrow morning. I would call the cops *then* if I was still feeling cranky.

I WAS LATE GETTING INTO work the next day, and Janet reminded me that my coworkers living in Maryland and Virginia managed to arrive on time, and my apartment was only a ten-minute walk away from the office. But people who lived in the suburbs were probably asleep by eleven, so how could I be expected to live up to those standards?

Our weekly staff meeting was about to start by the time I arrived, so I took an empty seat in the back of the conference room.

Everyone stopped talking when Janet walked into the room. A petite woman covered in freckles with a severe red bob haircut, she had a very loud voice for a woman of her size. She was always cursing and complaining, and everybody in the office seemed absolutely terrified of doing anything that might piss her off.

She started the meeting, going over some minor changes in the dress code. She told us that we could finally wear jeans during Recess, but none that were "embellished." (I snorted with laughter at this.)

"As all of you know, one of our LCs is leaving," Janet announced, "and we are currently looking for a replacement."

My ears perked up.

"Since nobody here has expressed an interest in the position, we're going to open it to outside applicants."

Nobody? What about me? I was more than qualified to write some wishy-washy form letters. I couldn't understand why I was being overlooked.

I asked Janet about it after the meeting.

"You're just not right for the job," she told me plainly.

And she left it at that, leaving me alone in the hallway to wonder why.

Perhaps I was being snubbed because I wasn't from the home state. Or maybe they knew how much time I spent posting goofy stuff on the Internet.

*Fuck it,* I decided. I didn't really deserve a promotion, did I? I was damn lucky to have a job at all. But there was no way in hell I would keep blowing my money on coke just so I could keep busting my ass in the mailroom. Jesus, what was I thinking?

Maybe this was a blessing in disguise. I loved drugs, but now I could go back to doing them just for fun, and I could finally start saving my money.

So I ran to the ladies' room to vomit. I had taken too much Valium on an empty stomach to cushion my come-down from the blow Sean and I did last night. When I came out of the stall, my eyes were red from puking so hard, and Janet was standing there, aghast at my appearance.

"Oh my God, are you okay?" she asked. "Have you been crying?"

I shook my head no.

"It's all right, Jacqueline, I know all about it. That guy is a jerk!" OMG, Janet thought I'd been crying in the bathroom over my "boyfriend" Dan. As if!

"Do you need to go to the nurse's office and rest for a while?" she offered.

"I can do that?" I asked.

"Please, take as much time as you need."

But I went back to my desk instead, embarrassed that everyone in my office thought I was a heartbroken fool.

I bought a new pair of Gucci shoes on the Neiman Marcus Web site to cheer myself up and waited for Happy Hour.


OUT OF LAZINESS, WE chose Capitol Lounge for Happy Hour. It was down the street from my apartment, an easy and convenient place to pick someone up on the way home from work.

We got a table next to a large group of deaf students from Gallaudet University. They were furiously signing to each other, and it looked like a pretty heated debate was going on.

"At least they're quiet," April joked.

"April!" I scolded her. "Watch what you say! Some deaf people can read lips, you know."

April picked up a menu and held it in front of her face.

"At least they're quiet!" she repeated.

"I heard you the first time."

"I bet *they* didn't!"

"April, sometimes you can be so du—Oh, never mind!"

The waitress delivered our drinks as the lights went down in the bar.

"Oooh, it's sexy time!" I announced. "Time to start thinking that the guys here are cute."

"I met Tom here," April admitted. "He looked my number up in the Senate directory and called me the next day."

"Aw, that's sweet."

"Yeah. Tom's a sweet guy."

April sighed.

"So why can't I stop cheating?" she asked, as if I were the expert on the subject. "I mean, I love Tom. But here I am, looking for Mr. Goodbar at Cap Lounge. Why do I do it?"

Every cheater asked herself this question whenever she felt guilty. But I wasn't going to let my friend beat herself up over something that was only natural for a woman who had options.

"Because love is not enough," I told her. "It just doesn't cut it anymore."

April thought on this.

"God, you are depressing," she finally said. "I need another drink."

"Yeah, but that's life," I replied.

"No, that's not life, that's just you being bitter. Most people don't feel that way."

"Yes, they do," I argued. "They just don't realize it."

April rolled her eyes.

"I can't believe we've been here almost twenty minutes and no one has bought us drinks yet," she complained. "We look really good!"

"I think the guys here are on to us," I said. "No one buys us drinks anymore because they know what stuck-up bitches we are."

"Well, we made our bed, I guess. We can either wait for new boys to come to town, or we're going to have to start wearing disguises or something," April surmised.

"This is bullshit," I said, getting up from the table.

I walked up to some random dude and tapped him on the shoulder.

"Can I buy you and your friends a drink?" I asked.

"Uh, sure!" the boy replied, amazed that a girl would even offer.

And that was all it took. Now we were the coolest girls on the Hill. All we had to do was throw some money around, and the guys loved us. Boys really weren't so different from girls in that respect. Male or female, we all loved free shit.

# Chapter 22

The next morning, I woke up with puke in my hair. But at least I was in my own bed.

I couldn't remember anything about last night, except that I had dropped my cell phone in a toilet. A men's room toilet. It was on my nightstand, right next to my hairbrush. Disgusting.

It was 9:15 in the morning. I was already late, but there was still time to get myself together and put in an appearance at work. *Eighty percent of success is showing up.*

I SAT AT MY DESK AND shuffled papers around, trying to look busy and important. After getting dissed yesterday, I was determined to get promoted to LC by the end of the year.

Obviously, I was meant for bigger and better things than sorting the mail.

I looked at the pile of mail on my desk and resolved to put all of my energy into my job. Starting tomorrow.

Suddenly, Janet burst into the room, shouting, "I need someone to take a meeting!"

I was the only one sitting in the Locker Room, since all of my officemates were at the four-hour fire extinguisher training course today.

"Jacqueline, you're not busy, are you?" she asked.

I supposed this was an opportunity to prove that I could do more than just open letters and look cute, so I agreed to take the meeting.

"Great! Just act like you agree with everything they say and you'll be fine," she told me. "Oh, and don't tell them you're a staff assistant! Tell them you're a legislative assistant or something, so they'll think that you're important."

"Who am I meeting with?" I asked.

"The Right-to-Life Educational Committee from the Catholic Diocese. Thanks so much for doing this! They're waiting in the front office."

*Fuck.*

Social issues usually don't affect me either way (which is probably why I'm a Republican), but the abortion thing . . .

What can I say? I needed one. Twice.

The first was during my "when-I-was-young-and-crazy-and-lived-in-New-York" phase. I was high or drunk most of the time, I didn't always use condoms, and I was always forgetting to take my Pill. Yes, I was fucking irresponsible (literally), and I wasn't exactly sure how long I had been pregnant because I had stopped menstruating during the months previous. I thought that all of the drugs and nonstop dancing had transformed my body into some sort of hyperthin, toxic fucking machine that could no longer carry on reproductive functions. Like I said, I was high or drunk most of the time, which also meant that I had probably done a lot of damage to the fetus. Obviously, I was not fit for motherhood.

The second one was under very different circumstances, when I was still with Mike. (And I was monogamous back then, so I can be certain that it was his, fuck you very much.)

We went on vacation and I forgot to pack my birth control. We got drunk on frozen drinks and I got pregnant. And that's when he proposed, but he didn't really want *me*, he wanted a family. So I pulled a Kay Corleone and told Mike that I had miscarried.

People like me just shouldn't have children. (We probably shouldn't be allowed to date, either.) If not for the freedom of choice, I would be raising a child somewhere, and how scary is that? A woman's right to choose is a right I hold as dearly as a woman's prerogative to change her mind.

Plus, I had no experience taking meetings with lobbyists, especially with nuns. I wasn't sure how to start.

"So . . . you guys are pro-life?" I asked.

"Why, yes, aren't you, dear?" one of them asked.

Should I represent the senator's office as a fraud or a baby murderer? If I wanted to keep my job, I would have to lie. I would have to lie to a nun.

Wasn't *everyone* in politics a goddamn fucking liar anyway? Perhaps this was my niche. I told lies all the time. Hell, I was *good* at it, a real bullshit artist. But part of me really wanted to tell these nuns to shove it. What did they know about abortions? Nuns didn't even fuck.

Marcus, a senior aide in my office, broke into the meeting.

"I'll take over from here," he said, much to my relief.

"Thank you!" I whispered as I gave him my seat at the table.

He smiled as he shooed me away.

*Nice guy,* I thought. *Too bad he's gay.*

I wondered if Marcus was "out" at work, or one of those right-wing closet cases. Not that it was any of my business. We all had our secrets, didn't we?

I went back to my desk, pissed that my office had put me in such a compromising situation. Wasn't it bad enough that I had all these abortions? Now I had to *lie* about it, too? I guess they just assumed that I wasn't the "abortion type."

I TOOK ALL OF THE antiabortion letters on my desk and put them in the garbage and began flipping through our office's copy of *Hustler* magazine. (Every office had a complimentary subscription.) I usually gave it to one of the Locker Room pervs, but only when I was done looking at it first.

A few minutes later, the door swung open and Janet walked in. She almost never came into the Locker Room unless it was to yell at somebody. I quickly threw the magazine into my desk drawer.

"Jacqueline, did you meet Marcus today?" she asked.

"He took the meeting with the nuns," I told her. "Am I in trouble?"

"No," she laughed. "He thinks you're hot!"

"Marcus is *straight*?" I asked without thinking.

The guys in my office, who overheard this embarrassing exchange, pealed into laughter.

"Many people have asked that question," Janet said, "myself included. But, yes, Marcus is straight and he thinks you're hot."

I glanced at my officemates, tittering to themselves at their desks.

"So this is what we're going to do," she continued, "after work today, the three of us are going to get a drink together. Does that sound good?"

"Sure, I'll go," I replied without hesitation.

I knew exactly what I was doing: gaining favor with Janet by entertaining her interest in playing matchmaker. Marcus didn't really seem like my type; neither had Dan when I first met him, but I was an open-minded girl. Maybe we would hit it off.

"Great!" she said. "I'll go tell him."

Everyone in the Locker Room burst out laughing as soon as Janet was gone.

"Don't you think that was weird?" one of my officemates asked me. "I can't believe she did that!"

"We're just getting a drink," I said casually, but I was aware that this seemed like a case of office politics gone bad.

"I think it's weird," he repeated, "but I want to hear all about it first thing tomorrow!"

At six o'clock, the three of us walked down the Hill to Union Station, where Janet was catching a train home in half an hour.

Janet and I ordered martinis, and Marcus ordered club soda.

"Marcus doesn't drink," Janet told me.

"Really? I don't know if this is going to work," I said half-joking.

"I was in rehab for three years," he told me.

*"Three years? For what?"*

I was fascinated by this.

"I'm just kidding," he said, laughing nervously.

*Damn.* So he was just another boring Senate staffer. The rehab thing made him so much more interesting.

"Why don't you drink?" I asked.

Perhaps it was a rude question, but I wanted to know.

"Alcohol isn't good for you," was his answer.

"Yeah, but it makes you *feel* good," I argued.

Janet wanted to change the subject.

"So, Jacqueline, where are you from?" she asked.

"I just moved here from New York a few months ago," I told them.

"Marcus is from New York!"

"Really? What part?" I asked. "I lived in Gramercy Park. Morningside Heights before that."

"Williamsburg," he told me.

"I shared an apartment on Bedford and North 7th one summer!" I told him.

So we had the Williamsburg thing in common. We were both pro-gentrification!

Pleased that Marcus and I had all that New York stuff to talk about, Janet left us to catch her train.

.   .   .

FIVE COCKTAILS (ALL ME) and four club sodas later, Marcus was walking me to my door. He didn't try to force himself inside my apartment like every other guy I had ever dated, nor did he ask if he could come in to use my bathroom. We worked together, so Marcus wanted to be careful with me. But I was too drunk to give a damn.

"Come in and see my apartment," I said, holding the door open for him.

He didn't hesitate once I had invited him inside.

"It's nice," he said, looking around, "but you need to get some furniture."

"I have some in my room. Do you want to see it?" I asked, beckoning him down the hall.

There was nowhere to sit, except for on the bed. (A decorating concept inspired by Dan's apartment.) I turned on my new television and flipped through the channels, looking for something appropriate to watch. Something that might showcase my good taste in television, but nothing too suggestive or anything that might distract us during a make-out session. I settled on a *Law & Order* rerun, for lack of anything better.

He seemed nervous, and I still wasn't convinced that he wasn't homosexual. I pounced on him, straddling his lap area.

Oh, he was straight.

I wondered if he would do the smart, sober thing and tell me to stop. I was drunk, so I had an excuse for my impetuous behavior. (That's why I drank so much in the first place.) But if Marcus wanted a boring girl, then I wasn't for him.

"You're trouble," he said. "I can tell."

"What do you mean?" I asked.

"I just have a bad feeling about you. You're trouble," he repeated.

"No, I'm not! I'm a nice girl."

"You're such a liar," he said, slapping my ass.

I giggled hysterically, so he started doing it really hard so it hurt. He rolled over so I could get him back, and I began waling on him mercilessly until he begged me to stop.

I leaned in to kiss him and he stopped me.

"Did I give you permission to kiss me?" he asked, spanking me superhard.

I was stunned. This wasn't your usual boring office fuck. This was far more intimate than regular sex: This was like blackmail material, and I loved it.

He left my apartment around one in the morning, leaving me to wonder why he didn't leave earlier, while he still had the chance.

# Chapter 23

"How was your date with Marcus?" everyone in the Locker Room wanted to know.

I wasn't sure why I felt compelled to tell them, but everything that happened in the Locker Room stayed in the Locker Room, right?

If I had heard that two of my coworkers were spanking each other, I would have filed it under TMI—too much information—and left it at that. Not that I wouldn't have found it *interesting*, I just didn't believe in giving anyone free publicity.

I guess I gave my colleagues too much credit, because it was a staffwide joke by the end of the day.

People on the Hill were the biggest gossips I had ever encountered: It was junior high with BlackBerries and Instant

Messenger. I learned my lesson that day: Do not talk about your sex life at work. (Unless you want to become extremely popular.)

*Writing* about my sex life was much more fun anyway, especially now that I had a new character—I mean, *person*—to write about in my blog.

I had just finished writing my first post of the day when Janet stopped by the Locker Room to speak with me.

"How did it go with Marcus after I left?" she asked.

I had a feeling that she had probably heard the spanking rumors.

"Good," I replied. "I really like him."

"Do you?" she asked. "Because if you *do* start dating him, you should know that when it comes to his personal life, Marcus is very discreet."

I nodded. This was obviously a warning to keep quiet from now on.

"And just so you know," Janet added, "the next time we have an opening for an LC position, I will certainly consider you."

This sounded promising: Instead of working harder, maybe I could sleep my way to the top.

"So would you go out with him again if he asked you?" Janet wanted to know.

"Of course!" I replied, and Janet went back to her desk.

About ten minutes later, Marcus sent me an e-mail, asking me out to dinner after work next week. Obviously, Janet had told him that I was receptive to a second date.

.    .    .

"OOH, HE LIKES YOU!" April said over lunch in the cafeteria that day. "And you like him, too, I can tell!"

"I do not!" I said, blushing. "He is *so* not my type! I mean, I thought he was *gay*, April."

"Why? Because he's good-looking? Because he's well-dressed? I'm surprised that you would be so prejudiced."

"I don't know. There's just something strange about him. Maybe he's bi."

"Oh, stop it, Jackie. Marcus likes women. He obviously likes *you*, at least."

"Yeah, because I'm *hot*," I chortled. "Sort of shallow, don't you think?"

April shrugged.

"No more so than anyone else we know," she replied. "Why are you being so judgmental anyway? There's nothing wrong with liking someone, Jackie."

I wasn't so sure if this was true.

"Yeah, but I don't *want* to like anyone," I admitted. "Marcus doesn't even drink, April. What am I supposed to do with him?"

"He wasn't drunk last night?" she asked.

"No," I replied, "he was totally sober."

"Wow," April said, "I thought people only did freaky stuff like that when they were buzzed."

"Yeah, me too," I agreed. "I wouldn't do half of the stuff that I do if I wasn't drinking."

"He must really like you."

"Oh, please! He was horny and I was drunk—end of story!"

"What if you guys got married? Do you think your senator would come to your wedding?"

"I've only known the guy for, like, five minutes, April! And what makes you think I would marry a guy like Marcus? Just because we both like spanking? Oh, that's another thing: He'll probably stop talking to me when he finds out about the rumor I started in the office."

"Yeah, that was a big mistake," April agreed. "I don't understand why you told anyone about that in the first place. Were you *trying* to start trouble or what?"

"Maybe I was," I admitted. "You know what he said to me last night? He said that he *knew* I was trouble, that he had a bad feeling about me."

"Maybe he's psychic," April surmised, "or maybe he loves drama just as much as you do."

"But I'm no femme fatale, I'm just the mailgirl! It's not like I can do anything to him except misplace his copy of *Roll Call* if I get pissed off at him."

"You could start an office sex scandal!" April reminded me. "Maybe that was just your passive-aggressive, messed-up way of sticking up for yourself."

"I guess that's what's bothering me about this whole thing. I feel like Janet was pimping me out and there was nothing I could do about it. But now I might actually like Marcus, so now I have nothing to complain about!"

"All's well that ends well, right?" April asked. "You'll probably have to make her a bridesmaid when you get married, though."

"I'm not sure if Marcus makes enough money for me. I

mean, he works *here*, after all. No offense," I said re April's boyfriend Tom.

"None taken. Maybe Marcus comes from a wealthy family like Tom does," she boasted. "Tom's father is a major contributor to the senator's campaign."

That explained how Tom got such a big job in his senator's office, and why April hung on to him all this time: He was the son of a rich campaign donor. In Washington, that practically made him *royalty*.


IF YOU HAD TO GET married, you should marry well, or else why bother? I thought Phillip was my most pragmatic choice for marriage at the time: He had the big house, the big dick, and millions of dollars. Why wasn't I all over it? It's not as if I could do any better than him. I mean, Phillip had it all.

That night, he was taking me to a fund-raiser. Since I was going as his date, no one had to know I was broke: When you were on the arm of a wealthy man, *you* looked like money.

But what to wear? I called up Laura for advice. Her new job took her to a lot of these Georgetown dinner thingies.

"Phillip is taking *you*?" she asked incredulously. "No offense, but people are supposed to take their *wives* to these things, not their young hottie girlfriends."

"That's bullshit," I argued. "I see older men with younger girls all the time!"

"Oh yeah? Where?"

"In New York."

"New York is different. People in Washington don't like gold diggers."

"Not true! What about all of those hookers at Café Milano?"

"Whatever, Jackie. You're going to a dinner at some rich old biddy's house. Just try to dress conservatively."

I put on my pearls and a black Diane von Furstenberg dress: a totally normal outfit, perfect for any occasion.

But I felt self-conscious standing next to Phillip in that room full of old people. I didn't like the way that people looked at us, passing silent judgment on our relationship.

"Would you mind if I leave you alone here for a few minutes?" Phillip asked me. "I saw someone that I need to talk to on the other side of the room."

Perhaps he felt as uncomfortable as I did, so I let him go. The bartender felt sorry for me, the stranded girl who was too young for this party. He kept my glass full, and I kept on drinking out of boredom.

I eventually gave up the patient girlfriend act and marched across the room to claim my date. I found him chatting up some drunk woman who looked like a goblin up close. She had a beak of a nose, funny lips, and bad skin. The thick layer of makeup she was wearing did nothing to cover the horrible craters all over her cheeks.

She was laughing at something Phillip had just said, putting her veiny hand on his shoulder.

Who was this monstrosity? And why did she look so familiar?

I stood next to Phillip, waiting to be noticed.

"It's my beautiful Jacqueline!" Phillip exclaimed, brushing the woman's hand away. "What are you doing over here?"

"I was looking for the powder room," I lied, smiling adorably. "Won't you introduce me to your friend?"

It turned out that this woman with a face for radio was actually a network news correspondent on *television:* Hollywood for the Ugly personified.

"Charmed," I said, offering my hand so that she could kiss it.

"Isn't she something?" Phillip chuckled. "Darling, let's do lunch sometime," he said to the woman as he pulled me into an adjoining room.

I assumed that he would scold me for "embarrassing" him or whatever, but instead, he kissed and groped me against the wall.

There were framed photos hanging next to my head, and the same man appeared in all of them. In one, he was fishing with the president. In another, he was golfing with the secretary of state. Whose house was this? Whosever it was, he had the ultimate Me Wall.

"Phillip! Are we supposed to be in here?" I asked.

He picked me up and threw me over his shoulder.

"Let's fuck on this guy's couch," he said, carrying me across the room.

"What if we get caught?" I fretted. "Every VIP in Washington is in the very next room! Wouldn't that be bad for your reputation?"

"That would be *good* for my reputation, actually. You know, there's no such thing as bad publicity."

We left the party drunk and giddy, skipping out on the

dinner in favor of more drinking at the aforementioned Café Milano. When I saw all the gold diggers catching Phillip's eye in their revealing cocktail dresses, I wished that I had worn something sexier after all.

"How did you like the party?" he asked.

"You call that a party? I can't believe you thought I would have fun with all those old—" I stopped myself, realizing that I was referring to Phillip's own peer group. "Except for those last fifteen minutes on the couch, I just had an awful time."

"I probably shouldn't have taken you there," he admitted, "but don't worry, we'll have a great time in South Beach."

Since I wasn't going home for Easter this year, I had agreed to go away with Phillip for the weekend. Going on vacation with a stranger was always a risk, but it was impossible to have a bad time in Miami. At the very least, I could get a cheap thrill from going topless, and a gorgeous tan while I was at it.

"So how do you know that creepy woman you were talking to?" I asked as our drinks arrived.

"Ugh, she's a horror show, isn't she? I see her at parties all the time. She's hot for me," he chuckled.

"Have you ever . . . ?"

"Noo! Do you know who she's married to?"

"Let's not order any food," I said, changing the subject. "Let's get the check and go back to your place."

No one really came to Café Milano for the food anyway. It was the place to see and be seen, "the cafeteria" for people who lived in Georgetown.

An aging brunette in a cleavage-baring dress stopped us as we made our way toward the exit.

"Is this the new one?" she asked Phillip, looking me up and down.

"Hello, Penelope," he replied, hustling me away from her.

We rushed out of the restaurant and went back to his house a few blocks away.

"Who was that woman?" I asked when we got outside.

Phillip told me the story of how she got pregnant on purpose, how she never really loved him, how he married her to do the right thing, how she got the big estate in Virginia, how she sold the estate for ten million dollars, how she still gets ten grand a month in alimony, how she got rich off of his life's hard work.

"I married a whore," he admitted. "She's the mother of my sons, but goddamn it, she's a whore. And did you see what she was wearing? What a slut!"

I wasn't sure what to say in response to that. Obviously, I didn't know enough about the situation to comment. I mean, Phillip had *children*?

I was small-time compared to a woman like Penelope, but what was the real difference between us? Why hadn't I been married and divorced yet?

Ah, yes: I had an abortion and she didn't.

So we went upstairs and fucked as if nothing had happened. It was the only thing we could do to make ourselves feel better. Phillip knew that he had nothing to worry about with me. After all, what he liked me to do, I couldn't get pregnant from.

# Chapter 24

I had a buttload of stuff to do before taking off for Miami that weekend. Besides packing and all that, I had a lunch date with Fred and a dinner date with Marcus. Then my ex-boyfriend Kevin actually had the balls to e-mail me, asking if we could get together while he was in town with his wife.

We had some unfinished business, so I agreed to see Kevin and cancelled on Fred, telling him that it was "my week off."

"Couldn't we just lay down a towel or something?" Fred pleaded over the phone.

"Ew, no!" I replied. "I hope you don't do stuff like that on a regular basis, Fred. That's, like, a biohazard."

"I thought *next* week was your week off."

How the fuck did he know? Was it on his Outlook calendar or something?

"Well, it came early," I lied. "That happens sometimes."

"But that's not supposed to happen if you're on the Pill," he argued. "You *are* on the Pill, aren't you?"

"No, I'm *trying* to get pregnant," I said sarcastically. "Of course I'm on the Pill! I don't want no fucking baby."

"I hate it when you talk that way, Jackie. It sounds terribly low class. I hope you don't talk that way to people at work."

I wanted to tell Fred to go fuck himself, but I didn't dare. You couldn't talk that way to the man who paid the rent unless you were his wife.

We rescheduled for next week, and I was free to meet Kevin at his hotel.

He and his wife were in town for some campaign law seminar at the J. W. Marriott, where they were staying.

"Maybe we could get a room across the street at the Willard," Kevin suggested, nervous that his wife might walk in on us.

I pretended not to hear him as I removed my clothes, throwing them on the floor.

"This has to be quick," he said, pulling down his pants.

I knew that Kevin liked doggie, so I bent over and waited for him to find the right angle, as men with not-so-large penises often had to do.

But I didn't really care if we fucked or not. I had already accomplished what I had come here to do.

My G-string was hidden behind his wife's Vera Bradley totebag, waiting to be found. And if she somehow missed it, then my sparkly Urban Decay body powder would do the trick: It was on Kevin's face, in his hair, and all over the bed.

If his wife truly loved Kevin, she wouldn't leave him over this. But if she wanted a divorce, I hope she got everything.

WHEN I GOT BACK TO MY desk, there was an e-mail from the Staff Ass in the front office. She wrote:

> Can you cover the phones for me this afternoon? I'm having a bad day. Thanks!

What was this shit?

Bad day?

*Please, bitch.*

I wrote back some bullshit telling her that I was superbusy doing my own job. If I was dragging myself to the office every day, pretending that everything was nice for eight hours, then everybody else had to do it, too.

Here's a secret: I hated my job.

But I was no quitter. I resolved to hang in there until I got promoted, since the only thing worse than having a job you hated was looking for another one!

Dating Marcus was a de facto promotion in itself: When you coupled up with someone on the Hill, you formed an alliance with them. I was somebody's girlfriend now, which made me a somebody by association.

In turn, the wild sex rumors I had started put an end to speculation about Marcus's sexual preference: He was a white heterosexual male, just like all of the other guys in the office. The legislative director couldn't call him a "fag" or "girl" anymore, because everyone knew that Marcus was banging the mailgirl.

Since we had already fucked, he didn't hesitate to invite me over to his house after taking me out to dinner that week. Nor did I hesitate to jump into bed with him as soon as he let me in the door.

We were totally hot for each other, and never once did he do anything I thought was creepy or misogynistic. So I had to know: Did he like anal?

"Not really," he said. "It's sort of unsanitary. Do *you* like it?"

I had never really asked myself that question.

I suppose I enjoyed the "nastiness" of it, but it was something I did only to please my partner, and it really depended on the size of their penis. It was counterintuitive, but the big ones hurt *less* than the small ones. (Less jabbing.)

"Do you want me to fuck you in the ass?" he asked me.

"Yeah," I told him. (He was big enough.)

"I want to hear you *say* it."

"What is this? Some sort of legal thing?" I asked.

"No, just *say* it."

I assumed the position, lifting my ass into the air.

"Please," I said, looking over my shoulder at him, "fuck my ass."

Instead, he rolled me over and kissed me on the forehead. I looked at him incredulously.

"Take it easy," he said, putting his arm around me. "There's nothing wrong. I just prefer regular."

I didn't know what to think.

I excused myself to the bathroom, and upon careful inspection, did not see (or smell) anything wrong. What kind of mind games was this guy playing?

I stalked back into the bedroom, ready to dispense my usual indifferent attitude toward the men I fucked, but I couldn't do it this time: I was so happy that I had found a guy who just preferred regular.

When I awoke the next morning, I wished that I wasn't leaving for Miami in a few hours. Then I realized I had to stop myself before I got in too deep. A millionaire with a huge dick wanted to take me to my favorite city, fuck my brains out, and buy me expensive gifts—but I wanted to stay in bed with Marcus and watch television all day instead?

What was I thinking? I was a smart girl, so I told Marcus that I was going home for the weekend and got on that plane with Phillip. I had to straighten up and fly right. (First class, of course.)

# Chapter 25

Why doesn't everyone just pack up everything and move it down to Miami? The government, the stock exchange, everything. We're all just going to end up moving down here when we retire anyway. Why not just get it over with? Or at least put a man-made beach in Washington or something.

I loved the beach. Everyone went topless in Miami, so you just had to take it off, or you'd look like an uptight bitch with body image issues.

It wasn't as if anybody was looking at me anyway. While I may have been a head turner in Washington, I was totally invisible here: There were fucking models everywhere! They were jogging on the beach, playing volleyball, and swimming in the ocean. I wished I were more the active type. At least it would give me something to do besides constantly obsess over my life.

Oh, yes, I knew that I was self-absorbed, and incredibly so. But if I wasn't paying attention to myself, who was? Phillip sure wasn't. It was as if he had brought me all the way down here just to ogle other women. He couldn't help staring at all the hot bods.

When I got up to readjust my lounge chair, a woman dressed in Helmut Lang approached me. Obviously, she was from New York.

"Would you like to be in our magazine?" she asked me.

I looked at her as if to ask, *Why me?*

"It's for *Glamour* magazine," she told me. "It's for our makeover issue."

"No thanks," I said, waving her away.

How dare she imply that *I* needed a makeover. As if I would want to pose for some awful "Before and After" pictures. How humiliating.

"Wait a minute!" I shouted after her. "How much would I get paid?"

"Nothing, but you would get to be in *Glamour* magazine!" she replied.

"Sorry, no thanks."

If I was going to be humiliated, I should at least get paid for it.

"You're a smart girl," Phillip said, taking my hand in his as I sat down. "That's why I love you."

"Whatever!" I said, snatching my hand away from him.

How dare he patronize me.

It started getting cloudy, so we went back to the hotel to

shower and change clothes for dinner. We were going to China Grill on a Saturday night, so I had to "do it up," as they would say in Bay Ridge, or else we wouldn't get a table.

I put on a bright green silk Diane von Furstenberg cocktail dress with a plunging neckline to show off my new tan. It was the perfect "arm candy" dress, and I had several like this one, all purchased in hopes of living a life that I had yet to lead. Mike never took me out anywhere, and it was too garish for Washington, so I was happy to finally have a place to wear it.

I blew my hair out straight and put on my big Kenneth Jay Lane bracelets and earrings. Going to Miami was like Halloween for us Yankee girls. You could really go OTT with the *bijoux* and no one would blink an eye.

I put on my gold strappy high-heeled sandals, and I was ready.

"You are gorgeous!" Phillip told me when I finally came out of the dressing area. "You should wear that dress more often."

I smiled as I took his arm. *This* was the life I wanted to lead.

DESPITE MY EFFORTS TO look as fabulous as possible, we still had to wait for a table at China Grill. The competition was fierce. Models, movie stars, athletes, even the nobodies looked like they were *somebody*. As I had noticed on the beach earlier that afternoon, every woman had breast implants and these perfect bodies to go with them. They wore Versace and tons of jewels and were not ashamed to be glamorous and sexual.

I just couldn't compete with women like these. Thank God I lived in DC, where I could let myself go and still get dates.

When we finally got a table, it was worth the wait: right in the corner, so we could watch the room. Phillip definitely had a wandering eye. Whenever he looked at me, I felt as if he was wondering how he might be able to trade up for someone just a little bit hotter, and I shifted in my seat. How humiliating.

Where was that cocktail waitress? I needed a drink ASAP.

As always, I felt better as soon as I had a few cocktails. Once I was drunk, it didn't bother me so much that Phillip liked to look at other women. So what? He couldn't help it. That's just what men did.

Besides, Phillip was taking *me* back to Washington tomorrow, so it didn't really matter who he wanted to fuck tonight.

Phillip had all sorts of interesting things to say when he was drunk, especially on the subject of marriage. I wasn't sure, but I thought Phillip may have been married more than once. His advice sounded so cynical.

"Never sign a prenup," he told me. "If a guy asks you to sign one, refuse to marry him. He doesn't love you."

I laughed at this.

"What if *we* got married?" I asked. "Wouldn't you ask me to sign a prenuptial?"

"I'm too old to marry you," he said.

I was somewhat disappointed to hear him say this, but it was true, and I had to respect anybody who could tell me the truth up front.

"I'm not sure I want to get married," I told Phillip.

"Of course you do," he said. "And if you're smart, you'll marry rich. You're a beautiful woman. You can do that."

I just couldn't marry *him*. At least I knew where I stood.

As we waited for the check to arrive, Phillip asked me where I might like to go "clubbing" afterward. Of course, I loved the nightlife as much as anyone else, but the idea of partying with such an older man made me cringe.

"I don't know, I'm getting pretty tired from all that laying out we did today," I lied.

"Well, I'm going without you," he said. "I'll put you in a cab so you can go back to the hotel."

"Uh, okay," I said, suppressing my rage.

I went back to the suite alone, cried for about twenty minutes, and changed into jeans and a T-shirt. I sat on the king-sized bed, wishing that I had come here with someone like Marcus. What was I even doing with Phillip in the first place? What kind of girl lets strangers pick her up off the street?

I realized that, for the last few months, I had been walking a very thin line.

Phillip was out until six in the morning, doing who knows what with who knows who. By then, I was already in Washington, back in bed with Marcus.

I WAS SO RELIEVED TO find him alone when I showed up at his house in the middle of the night, and he didn't ask for an explanation as to why I was back in town so early. He just assumed that I missed him—and I did—but there was still so much he didn't know.

That was one big difference between me and him: He wanted to believe that I was a good person, and I wanted to believe that he was just another asshole who wanted to fuck me over. That was the hell that cheaters created for themselves: I had to assume the worst about people because I knew firsthand what horrible things they were capable of.

Nevertheless, I was really an optimist deep down inside. Despite everything that life had shown me, I always believed in love: I wanted someone to take me away from these simple feelings I knew.

I was just another stupid girl waiting for Prince Charming to give me true love's first kiss, and I hated myself for it.

*Chapter 26*

When Marcus and I went back to the office on Monday, I ducked into an empty conference room to call up Fred and confirm our schedule for the week. He surprised me by inviting me out to dinner that night, which could have only meant one of two things: He either wanted to put an end to our arrangement, or else he was just getting careless.

I knew it was the latter when he held my hand across the table at La Colline, the fancy French restaurant on the Hill. It was as if he *wanted* to get caught. I looked around nervously, afraid that someone might see us.

"What's wrong?" Fred asked. "You look nervous."

"Aren't you worried?" I asked.

"Not at all," he smiled. "I'm just happy to get out of the house and see my pretty little girl tonight."

I frowned at this.

"What's wrong?" he asked.

I felt like I had to tell him. If Fred could have a wife, I could have a boyfriend, couldn't I?

"Are you sleeping with him?" he wanted to know.

"*Fred*," I blushed, "I don't ask questions about *your* sex life."

"That's because *you* are my sex life right now! If you're sleeping with other people, you have an obligation to tell me."

"Ha!" I laughed. "I don't remember taking any vows with you."

"Jackie, if we're having unprotected sex, you have a *responsibility* to tell me."

The people at the next table raised their eyebrows at us.

"Do I?" I asked. "There's no law that says that I do."

"Yes, you do, actually! You have a *legal* responsibility. If you give me a disease, I could sue you. There is legal precedent—"

"So sue me!" I chided him. "Do it, I dare you!"

We were officially "making a scene," so I stood up from the table and walked out of the restaurant.

I did not appreciate being threatened by lawsuits and accused of having STDs. Where was this coming from anyway? Was Fred *jealous*?

I walked home to let off some steam, ruining my Gucci heels. These were shoes meant for stepping in and out of limousines, not walking home alone.

It was only nine o'clock, but I was sick of this day. I went to bed early, thereby putting an end to it.

Of course, I couldn't fall asleep. I lay awake, wondering if I should call up Marcus.

Then I heard someone at the door and a key turning in the lock. It could only have been Fred. (He was the only other person with a key.)

I pretended to be asleep as he walked into my room.

What was he going to do? Kill me?

*Go ahead*, I thought. *Make my day.*

I said nothing as he took his clothes off and slipped into my bed. I lay motionless as he climbed on top of me and stuck it in. Apparently, Fred wasn't as worried about STDs as he pretended to be.

He kissed me goodnight and gave me another envelope before he went home. Fred had given me approximately $20,000 in cash since our arrangement started, but this was the first time I ever really felt like a whore. Up until tonight, I believed that I was just a very lucky girl who happened to be at the right place at the right time.

Yes, I had been walking a very thin line for the last few months, but not for nothing: I had a job, my own apartment, plenty of spending money, and more men than I knew what to do with—one of whom I actually *liked.*

Obviously, I was being rewarded for my behavior, and while my life wasn't perfect, I was getting what I wanted. Maybe I wanted all the wrong things, but I was so busy chasing after all of this shit that sometimes I forgot what the difference between right and wrong was in the first place.

.  .  .

AT WORK, THE SEX RUMORS had finally subsided, much to my relief. I felt awful for betraying Marcus's trust so early in our relationship, but he just shrugged it off.

"I knew this would blow over in no time," he told me. "People on the Hill are too busy obsessing over themselves to pay any attention to whatever we're doing."

"So you're not mad?" I asked.

"Are you kidding? This sort of stuff happens a lot more than you think," Marcus told me.

"Really? Like what?" I wanted to know.

"If I ever want to start a smear campaign, you'll be the first person I tell."

I rolled my eyes and called April on my cell. She wanted to meet Marcus, so I told her to meet up with us at Lounge 201.

This was major. (To me, at least.) I didn't bring guys around my friends very often. Why force them to talk to some jerk who I was only going to dump anyway?

But dump Marcus? Then I would have to find another job—no thank you!

"I've heard so much about you!" April said when I introduced them.

"Yeah, and so has everyone else," Marcus laughed.

"Oh, you know how us girls like to talk. We're terrible!"

The waitress came by to take our drink order.

"I'll have a club soda," Marcus said after April and I ordered wine.

"A club soda?" April asked. "Oh, right. You don't drink. Jackie wrote something about that in her blog."

I kicked her under the table.

"You have a blog?" Marcus asked me. "What do you write about?"

"Um, I don't really have a blog," I lied. "April was just kidding."

I shot April a look that said, *You'd better back me up here.* This slipup of hers could get me into big trouble.

"Yeah, just kidding!" April repeated. "I must have been thinking of someone else. Jackie doesn't have a blog! She's not a computer nerd or anything."

Marcus looked befuddled.

"If you have a blog, I'd love to read it," he told me.

"I do *not* have a blog!" I insisted. "If I had one, I would tell you about it, wouldn't I? It's not as if I have anything interesting to write about anyway."

I was such a fucking liar. But Marcus bought it. I kicked April under the table again when he went to men's room, extra hard this time.

"You bitch!" I hissed across the table. "Just what were you thinking?"

"Sorry! It just slipped!" she winced.

"He just forgave me for starting the spanking rumor! I don't want to push my luck!"

"Oh, don't worry, Jackie! You should see the way he looks at you. He just feels lucky that he found you."

"Lucky," I snorted. "Yeah, right."

Marcus was probably the unluckiest guy in the world. I was a vain, arrogant, selfish girl who lied and cheated her way through life—a train wreck of a person.

But he didn't have to know about any of that. He suspected that I was trouble, but he saw something in me and believed I was worth the risk.

I wanted to show him that he was right. Because I *was* worth it.

I LEFT THE BAR WITH Marcus, holding his hand as we walked up to the Capitol to watch the sunset. All the regular people had to be satisfied with their view from the ground, but we were special: We had ID.

*This is where we work*, I thought. *This is where we met.*

From the Capitol steps, we could see everything: the monuments, the memorials, the cherry blossom trees by the Tidal Basin.

God, what a beautiful city we lived in. You could really believe all that "shining city upon a hill" bullshit when you had special badges that allowed you to see things like this.

Every Capitol Hill couple needs to have that first kiss on the steps. Nothing could ever top that. *I will never have a romantic moment as perfect as this one for the rest of my life. I may as well shoot myself now*, I thought.

Sure, I could go back up there with some other guy and try to re-create the experience, but it just wouldn't be the same. There could only be one first time, and this was it.

What was I doing, standing up there with Marcus, holding his hand? Suddenly, I felt like the dorkiest dork in the USA. I had to get down from there ASAP.

"Jackie, what's wrong?" Marcus asked, running down the steps behind me.

"I have to pee," I lied.

"Hey, wait a minute!" he called after me.

I stopped and turned around to look at him.

"That is amazing!" he said.

"What's amazing?" I asked.

"How do you run so fast in those heels? I'm impressed!"

He was serious, and I don't know why, but I was flattered that he had noticed my prowess on high heels. It was probably the most sincere compliment that I had received in a long time.

I didn't know why it was so hard for me to like somebody. It wasn't so bad after all.

We started sleeping together every night after that. A week went by, and I realized that was the longest time I had been monogamous since my engagement to Mike.

I knew that seven days wasn't such a long time, but to me, it meant something: I was ready for this, and everything in my past, I wanted to let it go.

I stopped going out with my friends, telling them I was busy with Marcus whenever they called me up on my cell.

"Your friends are going to hate me," he said on our eighth night in a row. "Are you sure you wouldn't rather go out tonight? You're probably sick and tired of hanging around my boring house."

"Are you kidding?" I asked. "You've got HBO. Besides, I'd much rather hang out with you than get drunk and make out with some random DC date-raper."

"Is that what you do? In that case, you're never going out with your friends again."

"Well, my best friend, Naomi, is coming into town this week, and I'm taking her out whether you like it or not. She's staying with me, so I might not see you for a few days."

"I'll see you at the office, won't I?"

"I might call in sick while Naomi is here. Promise you won't tell Janet?" I begged.

"Unlike you, I can keep a secret," Marcus teased. "Just be careful when you go out."

"I've been taking care of myself for some time now, Marcus. Don't you worry about me."

# Chapter 27

That Wednesday, I took Naomi to Saki. She just had to see how ridiculous this place was, and by now, I had line privileges here, which meant only one thing: I had been spending way too much time in cheesy DC nightclubs.

It was April, Laura, Naomi, and me. And a couple of Laura's clients, two middle-aged men who looked totally psyched to be there. April was keeping them entertained by feeding them cocktail cherries.

"The deejay here totally sucks," Naomi complained as "Smells Like Teen Spirit" came on over the sound system. "Does anybody ever do drugs here or what? It looks like everybody here just likes to drink."

"I think we might be the only people doing drugs here," Laura told her. "Nobody's ever holding except us."

"What do you have?" Naomi wanted to know.

"All we have right now is coke," Laura replied.

"Wow. That is pathetic. Here, take a Vicodin," she said as she doled them out on the table indiscreetly. "That's the problem with you lame fucks in Washington. Not enough drugs!"

Laura looked horrified as her clients examined the white oblong-shaped pills. April smiled and popped one into her mouth, and they did the same.

"*Shit*," Laura muttered. "I am so fired."

"Don't worry, dear," Naomi told her, "they are going to love it!"

FOUR HOURS LATER, I was sitting on the filthy, disgusting sidewalk in front of Pizza Mart. My friends were sitting inside, eating big nasty slices of pizza. Even Naomi, who usually refused to eat any pizza that wasn't hand-tossed in the outer boroughs, had succumbed to the post-Saki craving for a Jumbo Slice.

The only thing more disgusting than eating one of these things yourself was watching *other* people eat them, especially the drunk ones. I sat there in my Marc Jacobs tank top and miniskirt, staring as people crammed oily wedges into their mouths.

Then I noticed a crowd forming around me.

What were they all looking at?

I realized that my underwear must be showing, but I didn't care.

Then I remembered that I wasn't wearing underwear.

Whatever. I still didn't care.

My friends collected me and put me in a cab.

"Capitol Hill," I told the driver. "Pennsylvania and Fifth Street, Southeast."

"Shit!" he cursed at me.

You would think that he would be happy that I lived so far away. Then he could charge me a higher fare, right? But I had no idea how these things worked.

DC had some crazy "zone system" for determining cab fares. I never bothered to figure it out. It sounded like total bullshit to me. Like, the zones seemed so arbitrary. I mean, how could you even tell what zone you were in? I thought that there should be signs all over the city to let people know, "YOU ARE NOW LEAVING ZONE 6. WELCOME TO ZONE 7."

I was telling the driver all this, but he didn't seem to appreciate my effort at making conversation, so I gave up. I leaned back into the stinky leather seat and closed my eyes.

"Don't fall asleep in here!" the driver yelled at me.

Startled, I apologized, "Sorry! Sorry!" and sat there, not talking, not sleeping.

I listened to some of the Nation of Islam radio show that he had playing on his radio and looked out the car window. We were driving through the "bad" part of town that no white people seemed to live in, a part of Washington that I had only driven through. It didn't look so bad, except there was no Starbucks.

"Have you ever been in this neighborhood before?" the driver asked me.

"No," I told him, wondering why he would ask.

"Do you know where you are?"

"Not really."

"Does *anybody* know where you are?"

Why was he asking me these totally fucked-up questions?

I noticed that the doors were locked, but then I felt like I was being racist for assuming that this guy meant me some kind of harm. Maybe he was just trying to make conversation?

I found my cell phone and called April, but she wasn't picking up. And neither was Naomi.

"No talking on the phone, damn it!" he yelled at me.

"Are you serious?" I asked.

He pulled over and got out of the car. What the hell was he doing?

I looked around for some kind of identification so I could get his name or something. When this was over, I planned to report this to the District of Columbia Taxicab Commission ASAP.

But there wasn't anything indicating that this was even a taxi at all. This was just some crazy dude's car!

"You and your cracker bitch friends think every brown face driving a car is your own personal limo service?" he asked, pulling me out of his car, which I realized was not a cab after all.

I thought about it. Had my friends just run up to his car, opened the back door, and thrown me in the backseat? And had I just barked out a destination when I got in? I guess that I had. But why had he not kicked me out of his car right then and there? Was he trying to teach me some sort of a lesson?

I was afraid to even look at him.

"I'm sorry," I said as my phone started to ring.

He frowned at me as he listened to my "Push It" ringtone. "Don't you dare answer that phone!"

"Sorry! Sorry!"

"You think you're so cute, don't you, in that ho outfit, walking around at four o'clock in the morning. Do your parents know where you are right now? You should be ashamed of yourself!"

I was stunned. Nobody—not even my parents—had ever spoken to me that way before in my life. My parents never disapproved of anything I had ever done because they loved me. But even so, I was grown: I could do whatever I wanted.

I looked down at what I was wearing. In total, my outfit must have cost upwards of a thousand dollars. But I had to admit, I did sort of look like a ho.

I was twenty-five years old, but I looked and sounded like one of those "out-of-control teens" on *The Jerry Springer Show*. Perhaps I still had some growing up to do.

Jesus, what a buzz kill. The man sped away in his car, ditching me in a neighborhood I didn't know. The streets were dark and empty, but not scary. I'd seen worse. Try the Marcy Projects at four in the morning. (Don't ask.)

I checked my voice mail, and a shrieking girl (Naomi) informed me that she was at the Grand Hyatt with some hockey players.

Why was I always the odd man out? People must have thought that I *liked* being alienated. Maybe they thought that it made me feel special or something.

*Fuck those sluts, they almost got me killed.*

Not knowing what else to do, I called Marcus.

Of course, he came to rescue me.

"Jesus Christ! What happened?" he asked as I climbed into the Jeep. "Are you high right now?"

"No!" I lied.

Marcus sighed.

"I won't tell Janet," he said. "Now tell me the truth. What are you on right now?"

"Vicodin," I admitted. "Have you ever tried it?"

"I don't do drugs, Jacqueline."

*"What?* You're lying!"

He shook his head no.

"You're thirty-five years old and you've never had a Vicodin?" I asked incredulously. "Get with it!"

"Good night, Jacqueline," Marcus said as he pulled up in front of my building.

"Aren't you coming in?" I asked. "I'm nice and relaxed from the drugs. You know what *that* means!"

He gave me a look that resembled pity.

"Get some sleep, Jackie. Call me when you're feeling better."

I got out of the car and watched him drive away, kicking myself for being such a slutted-out pill-head. That's what I was, wasn't I? No wonder he didn't want to come in.

. . .

THE GIRLS AND I WERE too tired to do anything later that day, so we parked ourselves at a table outside Signatures and watched the nightly dork parade march by on Pennsylvania Avenue.

The warm weather brought out the shirtless (male) joggers who shamelessly put their bods on display under the guise of cardiovascular fitness.

"This is amazing!" Naomi remarked. "Washington is, like, the gayest city ever. Look at them!"

A pack of shirtless men in brightly hued, high-cut running shorts bounded by the restaurant, panting and sweating.

"Hey, put some clothes on!" Naomi yelled after them.

"Naomi!" April admonished her. "You're embarrassing us!"

"So what? Do those guys really think that it's appropriate to run all over the city like that? It's disgusting."

"Exercise is just so *vulgar*," I agreed. "All that huffing and puffing. I can't believe people actually do it in *public*."

"I know what we should do! We should walk over to L'Enfant Plaza and look at the cute skater boys," April suggested.

We all agreed that this was the perfect low-energy way to spend our evening.

"These sidewalks!" Naomi complained as we started walking. "They're tearing up the soles of my new Loubous! Can we get a cab or something?"

"Let's just take the Metro," April suggested, pointing to the entrance of the National Archives–Navy Memorial station.

I forgot to tell Naomi the procedure for riding escalators in Washington. If you were lazy bitches like us, you were to stand on the right side of the escalator. But if you were a Type A asshole, you preferred climbing the stairs on the left.

One such busy and important person hit Naomi with his laptop case as he shoved her out of his way.

"Watch it, dicklick!" she shouted after him as he walked down the escalator.

"Stand on the right next time!" he yelled back.

"Like I give a fuck you're in a hurry! I'll fucking push you down the stairs, motherfucker!"

Didn't he know that you should never talk back to a New Yorker? Everybody in the Metro station stopped and stared at us: the people riding the escalator going up, the people buying farecards at the vending machines, and the Metro Police officer waiting for us at the bottom of the stairs.

He gave Naomi a citation for disturbing the peace.

"I'm never coming back here again!" she declared. "Fuck this fucking town and everyone in it!"

I WENT TO CHINATOWN with Naomi to keep her company while she waited for her bus to arrive that night.

"I wish you were coming back to New York with me," she said. "We could be roomies again, like that summer in Williamsburg. Wasn't that fun?"

"You know, Marcus is from Williamsburg," I told her.

She could tell by the wistful look on my face that I might be falling in love.

"Oh, my God," she said. "You *like* him!"

"Yeah, I think I do," I admitted.

"What are you, desperate? Isn't he a weirdo or something? I mean, you thought he was *gay* at one point, didn't you?"

"So what if he's a little strange? He's from New York."

"Can't you see what's going on here?" Naomi asked as the bus pulled up in front of us. "You're lonely in DC, so you fall for the first guy who treats you with even a scrap of respect in this town. Jesus, I thought you were smarter than that!"

She climbed on the bus, leaving me to wonder if she was right. Maybe I *was* desperate. How could I possibly be in love with Marcus? At best, I was merely infatuated and soon, the fascination would wear off. Then I would have to start all over again with a new boyfriend *and* a new job.

I went back to my apartment and lay in the bed, not knowing what to do with myself. I could imagine spending my entire life like this, lying alone in bed. It wouldn't be so bad. I could turn on the TV, watch whatever shows I wanted. I wouldn't have to listen to anybody snore, smell their stank breath, or listen to them complain about their boring job.

I could get a dog. As Harry Truman had put it, "If you want to have a friend in Washington, you should buy a dog."

And I could always masturbate whenever I wanted. That's one thing I had always really enjoyed, and I was good at it, too.

Nope, nobody cared about me, and I didn't care about them. Fuck everyone.

Then my phone rang. It was Marcus.

"Hey, where are you?" he asked.

"I'm running errands," I lied.

"Isn't it getting late? It's almost midnight."

Thank God. Another day closer to death.

"Do you want me to come over?" he asked.

Without hesitating, I said yes.

It must have been some irresistible biological urge to form a pair bond. Either that, or I really just liked the guy, and didn't want to end up alone, watching TV with my dog, masturbating.

# Chapter 28

There was no good way to end my arrangement with Fred. I felt like I was abandoning him in some way.

He obviously needed somebody to talk to, something to look forward to. Not only was I taking that away from him, I was taking that away from myself.

I couldn't fuck Fred during my lunch hour anymore if I ever hoped to have a normal relationship with Marcus.

I would have liked to stay friends with Fred, but I doubted that he would have wanted a nonsexual relationship with me. He already had one with his wife.

"Fred, is this still working for you? I mean, do you still enjoy this?" I asked him one afternoon at my apartment.

"Of course," he replied. "Why wouldn't I?"

I shrugged as he sat down on the bed next to me.

"What is this about?" he wanted to know, sliding my bra straps off my shoulders.

I shrugged again.

"So how's your new boyfriend?" he asked.

"I don't know. How's your wife?" I shot back, standing up from the bed.

He didn't answer.

"Stop asking me about Marcus," I said. "Don't make me sorry that I told you about that."

I stood there, hoping that he might want to give up on me if I started acting bitchy toward him.

"This isn't any fun anymore, is it?" I finally asked him.

"You're young," he said. "You still get to fall in love with people, but I can't."

"I didn't realize that you were paying me to stay single!"

I excused myself to the bathroom to get ahold of myself. Looking into the mirror, I thought to myself, *Jacqueline, you're fine. It's not your job to make other people happy.*

At least, not anymore.

I came out of the bathroom, determined not to let Fred affect me in any way. I was finally going to end it.

He grabbed me by the waist and kissed the top of my head.

"Your birthday is coming up, isn't it?" he asked.

I couldn't believe that he had remembered.

"I bought you something," he said, "but it's a surprise."

It *was* a surprise. I was impressed that he remembered my birthday. That meant I had to see him again, didn't it?

Wasn't it the right thing to do? What had I decided on before? Fuck, I couldn't tell right from wrong anymore. It was all getting so confusing.

I had to look at the bottom line: free gift (probably an expensive one), and another envelope of cash. I could let it go just awhile longer. What was one more week? We were both going to burn in hell anyway, right?

I agreed to meet him on the afternoon of my birthday, at our favorite place, the Hotel George. He said that we could get room service, with champagne and everything.

Who ever asked him to be so nice anyway?

I had dinner plans with Marcus for the night of my birthday, so April and Laura took me to the Palm the night before.

"I'm quitting my blog," April announced over dessert. "I think it's making me do crazy things just so I can write about them, like cheating on Tom."

I knew exactly what she meant.

"Every time I do something, I think to myself, *Is this blog-worthy?* It's a sickness," she said.

"Yeah, I should probably quit, too," Laura agreed. "I haven't posted anything in weeks anyway. My new job is crazy. In the private sector, you actually have to *work* for a living. God, I miss the Hill!"

"But don't quit your blog, Jackie! I need something to read when I'm bored," April told me.

I frowned, resenting the idea that my life had become entertainment for people. What if I ever got serious about somebody and settled down? Then what would I write about? How fat my ass was getting and what TV shows we liked to watch? Boring life, boring blog.

"We should try to make money off of your blog somehow," Laura suggested. "Like run ads on it or something."

"I don't know," I told her. "It's really not all that interesting, is it?"

"Sex sells," April reminded me. "You know that!"

I rolled my eyes.

"Then we would have to promote it in some way to get hits and stuff," I complained. "We'd have to prepare some sort of a business plan. I don't really want to get into all of that right now."

"But it could lead to other things!" Laura argued. "You could get your own newspaper column, or a job at a magazine. Do you really want to spend the rest of your life shoveling mail on the Hill?"

I shrugged. I hated my job, but if it meant that I got to see Marcus every day, then it didn't seem so bad. Of course, I would never admit this to my girlfriends: I had an image to maintain.

"I guess that would be cool," I said, "but I'd want to change it up a little first. It's much too embarrassing for public consumption."

"No, I think you should leave it exactly as is," April argued. "I think that people would relate to its honesty."

"Maybe, but wouldn't I get in trouble at work? And what about Marcus?"

"Your name isn't anywhere on it," Laura said. "If anybody finds out that it's you, just deny, deny, deny. Your office wouldn't want to make any noise over this, either—bad publicity. You would have them between a rock and a hard place."

"I can't fuck over my office like that. Just forget this crazy idea."

"Oh, come on! It would be fun!" Laura pleaded. "You should just go for it!"

"You're the only one of us who has the balls to do something like this," April told me. "What do you have to lose?"

They were serious about this. Did they not even care that I had a life here, too?

"I like my life just the way it is," I told them. "Besides, if we were serious about doing this, we'd have to do it right: We'd sleep with as many people on the Hill as possible and make them do all sorts of pervy stuff to us. We'd get them to tell us their secrets, any fantasies they might have, and then we'd post the stories and embarrass the shit out of everyone!"

"It would be pandemonium," April surmised. "The government might even have to shut down for a few days!"

"We totally have to do this!" Laura enthused.

"I was only kidding," I told them, "but if you guys like the idea, please feel free to use it!"

Just then, my cell phone rang. It was Marcus, asking if I needed a ride home from the restaurant.

"He wants to come over tonight," I clucked.

"You're either going to marry him, or you're going to end up quitting your job," April surmised. "Those are really the only two foreseeable outcomes."

"Don't be such a Cassandra," I told her, but I knew she was right.

I thanked the girls for dinner and waited outside, trying to imagine what married life would be like with Marcus, but I wasn't getting any pictures. All I could see in my mind's eye was the look on Mike's face when I came home from my rendezvous with Kevin. It was an omen of disappointment in my future.

My phone rang again. It was Dan, of all people. We hadn't spoken in weeks.

"What are you doing?" he asked. "Can I come over tonight?"

"Uh, I don't think so," I replied.

"Why not?"

"I don't need to be fucking the same guy as another girl."

I told him that I knew about Laura, the intern, and his bad reputation on the Hill.

"What, are you jealous?" he asked.

"Oh, Dan. Don't be so provincial," I sniffed.

He laughed at this, but I was serious.

"So we can't hang out anymore?" he asked.

"Well, if we're not fucking, then there's really no point in hanging out, is there?" I replied. "Besides, I'm seeing some-body in my office."

I explained what had transpired since our last con-versation.

"Your office sounds really screwed up. You should be very careful about dating someone who you work with," Dan warned me.

Of course, he would know.

We hung up as Marcus pulled up in his Jeep. As always, he got out of the vehicle, opened the passenger-side door for me, and we held hands the whole way to my apartment.

*This* was the life I wanted to lead, but tomorrow, I was meeting Fred at the Hotel George.

.   .   .

HE HAD BOOKED THE "Romance on Capitol Hill Package" that came with a bottle of Pol Roger Brut in the room. I owed him the courtesy of keeping this date, despite the fact that I had had morning sex with Marcus just a few hours earlier. This *had* to be the last time, because I couldn't keep this up much longer.

*Just one more time, and that's it,* I told myself.

I had said this so many times, about so many different things in my life. But this was the first time I actually meant it.

"Is something wrong?" he asked while he stuck it in.

"No, it feels good," I told him.

"Something seems different. I don't think you're getting wet."

"I'm, like, fine," I told him, but something *was* different.

I couldn't stop thinking about Marcus and how *wrong* this was. I was doing Fred such a favor, wasn't I? Drinking the champagne he bought me, letting him eat me out, taking his money afterward. Oh, and the Hermès scarf he bought me for my birthday? I only took it because I was just trying to do the right thing by *him.*

I wished that things could have been different for us: We were both such unhappy people. But now I had Marcus, and Fred would always have plenty of new girls to choose from in this town.

# Chapter 29

I showered and went back to my office, ready to put in a solid afternoon of data entry. I sat down at my desk to find an Instant Message from April:

> OMG you're famous!
> washingtonienne is on blogette!

I immediately began to shit myself.

One mouse-click on Internet Explorer opened Blogette.com. (I had set it as my homepage.) This is what it said:

## A Girl After Our Own Heart
### (She's So Getting a Book Deal Out of This)

This didn't seem like such a bad thing. I read on:

> Our sources say that Washingtonienne works for a
> senator from the Midwest . . . and we couldn't be
> prouder.

Then I saw it in blue hypertext. The link to my blog.
*Fuck.*

One more mouse-click and I was staring at "The Washingtonienne" as I had never seen it before: through the eyes
of a stranger.

These things that I had written in such humility for my
closest friends were suddenly being read by all sorts of
strangers and I couldn't stop them. The spanking, the anal
sex, the questionable exchange of money. My mind raced.

I had kept my Blogger Dashboard minimized for easy
access, so I could post at will. One mouse-click on the
"CHANGE SETTINGS" icon, then one mouse-click on the
button that said "Delete This Blog" (*hell yes!*), and my blog
was gone.

But it was too little, too late.

It was just a matter of time before some dutiful nerd
took it upon himself to re-post the thing. That was a given.
But then what?

Guessing the identity of "The Washingtonienne" and
her male cohorts might turn into some Capitol Hill parlor

game (played via Instant Messenger, of course), but *my* name would never come up: I was a nobody here. Maybe no one would find out, maybe nothing would happen.

Obviously, this was just my wishful thinking: I did not want to believe that my life could slip away from me like this, over something so fucking stupid.

Then the office door flew open.

It was Janet.

She stood in the doorway, glaring at me.

Suddenly, I was confronted with a hard copy of my blog. Janet held it up in front of me, scowling.

I stared at it in disbelief. I had never seen it printed out on paper like this before. How weird was it that *Janet* had a copy and I didn't? It was like something out of a bad dream, like the ones we all had about going to school and realizing that you're naked.

I couldn't even look at it, I was so ashamed.

"YOU PIECE OF SHIT!" she began yelling. "YOU ARE THE SORRIEST EXCUSE FOR A HUMAN BEING I HAVE EVER MET! YOU BETTER HOPE I *NEVER* CATCH YOU OUTSIDE OF THESE BUILDINGS!"

I didn't dare laugh at the idea of Janet jumping me on the street. It was obvious that Janet hadn't come in here to talk—she came in here to scream at me, but the least I could do was cooperate with the office and help with damage control.

"Janet, what should I do?" I asked.

"IF I WERE YOU, I WOULD START PACKING MY SHIT NOW BECAUSE I AM GOING TO MAKE DAMN SURE THAT YOU GET THROWN OUT OF HERE ON YOUR ASS! YOU WILL NEVER WORK IN THIS TOWN AGAIN!"

*Well.*

I wasn't waiting around for *that* to happen.

I picked up my cell phone and dropped it into my handbag.

And that was it. My shit was packed, so to speak.

I gave my office a chance. If this was how they wanted to handle it, by sending Janet in here to curse me out, then that was their mistake.

They could take everything from my desk and put it in the Smithsonian, because I was going forward with the plan that the girls and I had drawn out yesterday.

*Those fucking bitches.*

I click-clacked my way down the marble corridor toward the nearest exit, half-expecting somebody (please God, not Marcus) to come running after me, but that didn't happen.

Marcus. I could not even imagine what he must have thought of me. He was probably reading my blog right now, feeling as if he'd been duped. Surely, everyone I knew felt that way about me, because I really was a liar and a whore, and now I was exposed.

I was surprised that they would just let me walk out of here like this. I imagined this potentially turning into a *No Way Out* type of situation where "henchmen" might hunt me down to ensure my silence. At that moment I would have been highly susceptible to intimidation. I would have moved out of the country, changed my name, whatever they wanted. You would think they might have had some sort of protocol for these things, but I guess not. They let me walk out of there without so much as a word.

Right now, I was hardly the trash-talking bitch on wheels who wrote the blog. I was a frightened, lonely girl who was all dressed up with nowhere to go.

SO WHAT TO DO NOW? I'd go find April, since she was one of the evil geniuses behind all this.

I re-entered the Senate office buildings, wondering if there might be an APB out on me, but it didn't seem like it. The security guards flirted with me, as usual. Despite this life-shattering emotional trauma, it was nice to know that I still looked hot.

I stepped into the elevator, wondering if the people around me knew anything about my blog. I mean, not everyone on the Hill read Blogette as obsessively as my friends and I did. Maybe this was just a dirty little secret that my office would try to cover up. Couldn't they do that sort of thing? Wasn't a Senate office supposed to be powerful or something?

"FUCK YOU," the elevator doors read as they closed.

Ah. The same elevator I had taken up to April's office on my first day on the Hill. I should have known.

April looked very worried to see me standing in the doorway. I felt uneasy here, so I waved her over to the door.

"Oh, my God, April," I whimpered. "I've been fired."

Her face fell.

"They know already?" she asked, realizing what had happened.

I nodded, unable to speak.

"You need a drink," she said, walking me out of the building.

I needed about *seven* drinks that afternoon.

"Where will I go? What will I do?" I asked April at the nearest bar.

I don't know why I was asking her this question again. She was the one who suggested I should move to Washington in the first place.

"This is the craziest thing that has ever happened to anyone I know," April said. "I'm amazed at how well you're handling it. If it was me, I'd be in the hospital right now."

"Maybe I'm still in shock or something," I guessed. "I just don't know how to feel about any of it yet."

"It's probably a good thing that you've had a lot of fucked-up experiences behind you, or else you'd be totally unprepared for this level of trauma. But look on the bright side: This might turn into a great opportunity for you. You should be happy!"

"Are you serious, April? Call me crazy, but I'm not. I lost my job, my boyfriend, *and* it's my birthday. I am so *over*."

I looked at her, waiting for a confession.

"Was it you?" I finally asked.

"*What?*"

"Did you send Blogette the link?"

"No!"

I searched April for some sign of guilt, but was too drunk to pick up on it if there was one.

"If you tell me the truth, I'm not going to hate you," I promised. "I mean, I need all the friends I can get right now."

I didn't know what to think as I watched April's eyes fill with tears. She obviously felt sorry about *something*. I was tempted to grab her and say, "It was you, April! I know it was you. You broke my heart. You broke my heart!" like Michael Corleone in *The Godfather II*.

"Jackie, I'm serious. I wasn't the one," she lied.

I suspected that she wasn't being truthful, but it didn't really matter anymore, did it? This was my problem—*I* had created it. And I deserved everything—good or bad—that happened to me as a result.

"You know what, April? I don't care who did it. I am going to live through this," I said, "and as God is my witness, I'll never be sober again."

Then April hugged me, and I knew it was her. I also knew that she hadn't been trying to destroy me: She thought she was acting as my fairy godmother, that this would be my Cinderella story. But did she ever stop to think?

No, of course not. And neither did I.

"What are you going to do now?" April asked.

"I have no idea," I said.

"Should I go back to the office, or do you want me to stay with you?"

"Go back to the office," I told her. "Find out what's going on, and call me if you see my name mentioned anywhere. Hopefully, it won't come to that."

"Will do. And I'm coming over to your place after work. I don't think you should be alone."

"Why?" I asked. "Do you think someone might try to kill me?"

"I'm not trying to scare you, but you just don't know what people are capable of."

I had just made more enemies in one afternoon than most people made in a lifetime—it seemed anything was possible.

APRIL WENT BACK TO THE office, and I walked down to the Mall, which did nothing to improve my mood. The Mall looked so much prettier from the Capitol steps, away from the crowds of tourists on the ground. Where did this fat, classless segment of the American population with no fashion sense or sex appeal come from? I suspected they were the same people writing all those fuck-wit letters to the senator. I hoped they'd all die in a hotel fire.

My phone rang and I sat down on a bench to take the call. It was from an area code back home, probably from someone who wanted to wish me a happy birthday.

It was my mother.

"Did you get the birthday check I sent you?" she asked when I picked up.

"No, I haven't yet," I told her. "Did you know where to send it?"

"Lee gave me your address. She tells me that you're working for a senator in Washington."

"Yeah," I told her.

That was all I could come up with. I didn't know how to begin explaining what had happened to me today.

"Jackie," my mother began, "your father and I—"

"Yeah, I know," I said, cutting her off. "You're divorcing."

"I'm packing right now."

"Where are you going?"

"Jackie, I'm sorry to tell you this," she began.

I felt a stinging sensation growing inside my head as she told me that she was moving in with her boyfriend and that they were getting married in Nantucket this summer.

"You already have a boyfriend? And you're *marrying* him?" I asked. "Are you sure this isn't a rebound thing?"

My mother explained that she had been having an affair with this man for the last three years. Part of me was disgusted with her, but more so, I was disgusted with myself because I realized that I was just like her: I had become my mother.

Or maybe she was trying to be like me—I couldn't tell anymore. It was like the chicken and the egg in our case.

"What about Dad?" I asked.

My poor father. How could she do this to him?

"Jacqueline, your father is the one who threw *me* out," she told me.

"So I'm supposed to feel bad for you?" I balked. "You cheated on him!"

"You're not *supposed* to feel bad for anyone, Jackie! The only two people who really understand what happened are your father and I."

"I want to come home," I said. "I want to see you."

"Jackie, I'm going to the Cape for a few weeks, but I'll call you when I get back, darling. And then I'll visit you in Washington, and we can go shopping."

"Shopping? No, Mom, I want to come home."

"This is between me and your father, Jackie. You stay in

DC, go to your job, and have a good time with your friends. We want you to be happy, okay?"

I wanted to tell her that my life in DC was over, but she had enough problems of her own. I didn't know what else to say, so I said, "Okay," just for the sake of ending the conversation.

I had never been the homesick type. I felt like I was going backward whenever I went home, so I always avoided it. But now that I wanted to go back, I couldn't.

It was worse than Twilo closing.

I leaned back on the bench and closed my eyes. The sun shone orange through my eyelids.

*How rude,* I thought. *I hate the fucking sun.*

IT WAS DARK OUT WHEN I awoke. I jumped to see a homeless man sitting next to me on the bench.

"Can I tell people that we slept together?" he cackled.

I ignored him, as I often did the bums in my neighborhood. There was one on every bench and every street corner, begging for money. It was worse than New York because the homeless in DC were so belligerent.

You could be in the middle of a serious conversation with somebody, and they would interrupt, "Excuse me, Miss! Excuse me! Excuse me!" And you would think it was something important, like you were about to walk into traffic or something. So you would stop to see what it was, only to learn that the guy just wanted a quarter. Then you'd tell them no, and they would get all pissed off and call you a "rich honky bitch" or whatever.

I mean, so rude! And if you ever *did* give them money, they would stalk you on the way to work every morning, expecting you to give them money every day for the rest of your life.

I learned a valuable lesson living here: *If you want to keep money in your pocket, never be nice to anyone.* Or in other words, if you wanted to be rich, you had to be bitch.

When I got back to my apartment, I saw two pink envelopes sticking out of my mailbox: One was the birthday check from my mother, and the other was a birthday card from Diane.

On the front was a picture of a snobby-looking white Persian cat with a wee, cat-sized crown on her head.

Inside, the card said:

Happy Birthday, You Drama Queen!

And beneath that, Diane had written:

Here's to another year of living vicariously through you!

Was this a joke? Why would anyone want to live vicariously through *me*? My life was shit. The only good thing about it was Marcus.

The thought of him made my heart ache. He had given me his love and trust, and I stabbed him in the back. Of all the bad things I had ever done in my life, I feared this was the one that would plague me.

But tonight I could only worry about myself. I still had no indication of how out of control this blog thing might get, but I knew I had enemies, and Marcus was probably one of them.

As promised, April came by after work, and she had stopped at the liquor store on the way over.

"Another drink, and you won't miss him anymore," she said as she poured me a tall glass of Southern Comfort.

"I'm supposed to be having dinner with him right now," I sighed.

"Well, there's been a change of plans."

We clinked glasses and chugged our drinks.

THE NEXT MORNING, we were lying on my living room floor, surrounded by empty bottles and cigarette butts, when my phone started ringing.

"Jesus fucking Christ, what time is it?" April complained.

I scrambled to find my cell.

It was eight o'clock in the morning, and the caller ID showed a phone number with a 224 prefix, which meant that it was coming from a Senate office.

"Oh my God, they're calling me!" I shrieked. "What should I do?"

"Don't pick up!" she warned. "If they have something important to tell you, they'll leave a voice mail!"

We waited for my Salt-N-Pepa "Push It" ringtone to end.

Then Jay-Z's "Dirt Off Your Shoulder" started to play.

"Ha!" April laughed. "That's the ringtone for your voice mail? Cool!"

"How rude of them to call so early," I scoffed. "They should have known I'd have gone on a bender last night."

We listened to the message:

"Jacqueline, this is Janet from the office. It is extremely important that you call me right away. Thank you."

"Should I call her back?" I asked April. "Or should I get a lawyer first?"

"Do you have one?" she asked.

I thought about this.

"Phillip is an attorney. Do you think I should call him?"

"Didn't you write about him in the blog?"

I remembered that I had. Nasty stuff, too.

"Then you don't want to call Phillip!" April warned. "Isn't he some sort of legal mastermind? He could sue the shit out of you!"

"What for?" I wondered. "I don't think anyone has grounds for a lawsuit. I didn't use any names, so reasonable expectation wouldn't apply."

"What about privilege?"

"Ha," I laughed. "There's no such thing as 'top-bottom privilege,' is there?"

"But you never know, somebody might make up a reason to sue, like 'emotional duress' or whatever."

"They can sue me all they want, but I'm sure none of them would risk outing themselves. They wouldn't get a dime anyway. I'm unemployed!"

My phone rang a second time.

"Oh, my God! They're calling me again!" I gasped.

"They're sweating you," April laughed. "Let it go to voice mail."

We listened to the second message:

"Hello, Jacqueline. This is Janet from the office. I just want you to know that you are on paid leave, but I need you to call me back right away. Thank you."

"Now she's panicking," April observed. "She's probably afraid she'll get fired for scaring you away yesterday."

"Well, she should be," I said. "I mean, the *ego* that woman has, thinking she can act like that and get away with it!"

I realized that people were probably saying the same thing about me, but so what? This was America: I had the right to be an immature, hypocritical jerk if I wanted to, and if I was getting fired for it, then maybe Janet should too.

"Why are they putting me on paid leave?" I wondered. "Why don't they just fire me?"

"Paid leave means that you're still an employee, so you're probably not allowed to talk to the press or anything."

"Why would I want to talk to the press?"

April shrugged.

"Phase two of the plan?" she suggested.

The plan.

I *wished* I had a plan. All I knew was that I wasn't going to the office today.

"Let's just wait and see what happens," April told me. "People have short attention spans. This thing might just blow over."

It was eight thirty in the morning, and despite her hangover, April was going into the office so that she could report back any updates on the blog situation.

An hour later, April called me from work with some bad news.

"Everybody here is talking about it!" she whispered over the phone. "It's all over the Staff Ass message board! People know that it's you!"

Apparently, people on the Hill were playing on the Internet instead of doing their work. How totally shocking.

"Is my name out there?" I asked anxiously.

"Yeah, and there's a picture, too," April told me. "It looks like a yearbook photo or something."

This was just getting worse and worse.

"My life is over," I groaned. "Nothing will ever happen to me again."

"Don't feel bad!" April insisted. "It would have happened sooner or later, and all these losers on the Internet are giving you all this free publicity! You should be happy!"

April was really giving herself away, telling me to be happy as my life fell apart, live over the Internet. She was doing the right thing by helping me through this, but for all I knew, she was the one who put my name and picture out there. I just couldn't trust anybody anymore.

"Now that your name and face are all over the Internet, you've got nothing to lose," April offered.

"Is it a good picture at least?"

April hesitated, so I could tell that it wasn't.

"Can you e-mail it to me so I can at least see what it looks like?" I asked. "Maybe I can figure out where it came from."

When I opened the link that April sent me, I could barely recognize the girl in the photo. She looked like a child, with a round face and a funny-looking ponytail. It must have been taken during my tomboy years at Syracuse.

I will never know why one of my college classmates would go to the trouble of scanning my photo and sending it to all these freakazoid Web sites. It was obviously someone I knew, who stood next to me at alumni receptions, and they wanted to participate in my humiliation for reasons I didn't understand. I guess they were just bored at work, like I was.

Apparently, there were a lot of bored people in DC who didn't feel like doing their jobs, or else the news wouldn't have spread so quickly.

The Internet was *the* forum for opinions that nobody asked for, hence the abundance of Web logs like mine. Blogs are a great way for us self-absorbed exhibitionists to exercise our First Amendment rights. But I didn't write about my sex life to outrage anyone or piss off the girls who read it; I was actually trying to keep an account of my actions. Instead, it just became this shocking tabloid thing.

# Chapter 30

Late that night, I got a phone call from a number I didn't recognize. Of course, I let the voice mail pick up.

"Hi. It's me," a man's voice said. "Listen, I just have to say—and I'm not calling to yell at you—this is a *very* painful thing for everybody involved, and I'm sure, especially for you. I— I don't know what's going on. I don't know what you're doing here. But I'm just going to give you some friendly advice because I think you're a nice person.

"You need to move on with your life. You need to get this behind you and just move on, and forget about it, and not talk to anybody about it, and not write about it, not go forward with it. You just need to *move on*. It's better for you, it's better for everybody. You've been hurt, people have been hurt, I've been hurt, a lot of people have been hurt. Just do the right thing. You don't want to go in this direction. You know I— I feel bad. I feel bad for me. I feel bad for *you*.

"I wish you the best, I really do. And, um, it's just a very sad thing. And you've just— you've got to *move on*. Bye."

I played the message again for April.

"It's obviously Dan," she concluded. "Who else would leave such a bitch-ass message?"

"He sounded scared, April."

*"He's* scared?" April scoffed. "Don't worry about him, Jackie. He's an asshole, remember?"

"Yeah, but he's right, I need to move on," I admitted. "I'll go back to New York and move in with Naomi—I can leave Washington just as easily as I came, and I'll forget this even happened."

"You can't just run away," April argued. "You shouldn't be forced to move out because of this rubbish—you need to stay here and show people that you're not ashamed!"

"People? What people?" I asked. "Just who am I trying to impress here?"

"It's not about *impressing* anyone—it's about coming out of this a winner."

"But I'm *not* a winner—I'm a total screwup! I don't deserve to get anything from this at all."

"Not true! Everyone deserves success—everyone deserves to be *happy*. It's, like, in the Bill of Rights."

"Actually, we're only entitled to the *pursuit* of happiness."

"Well, that's bullshit."

April looked at the sweatshirt I was wearing, which I hadn't taken off in days.

"*Fordham Law?*" she asked. "Did you get that from Marcus?"

I nodded.

"Take that shit off," she scolded me. "You can't let these guys get into your head. If any of them still cared about you, they'd be trying to help you right now."

I supposed April was right. It was every man for himself.

THE NEXT DAY, I GOT a FedEx from the senator's office. It was the letter I had been waiting for all week.

*Ms. Turner:*

*As you know, we have been trying to contact you since early on the morning of May 19. We had hoped to discuss this issue in person, but since you have not returned our calls or come in to the office we have no option but to send you this letter instead.*

*On the afternoon of May 18, our office became aware of allegations that you had been using Senate resources and work time to post unsuitable and offensive material to an Internet Web log. After investigating these allegations the office finds that your use of your office computer, and other materials associated with that computer, was unprofessional and inappropriate, and that these actions are unacceptable.*

*Accordingly, effective May 21 your employment with this office is terminated . . .*

I totally agreed: My actions were unacceptable, and I deserved to be fired. But I objected to what they had said about my blog, calling it "unsuitable and offensive material." I mean, this was my *life* they were talking about: Was there really such a thing as an "unsuitable and offensive" lifestyle? It seemed like a very un-American thing to say.

I guess it was officially over. I did something terrible and got punished for it. The End.

But I was still here, with nothing to do, no place to go, and nobody to talk to.

When I called home, no one picked up. But what would I have said anyway? My parents already had enough drama in their lives, with the divorce and everything—they didn't need to hear about this bullshit. If this thing was just going to die out anyway, then I didn't have to bring it up to them just yet. I could tell them over Thanksgiving dinner or something.

I went outside, wondering if anyone in my neighborhood might recognize me, but no one said anything if they did. It seemed like whatever hostility people felt toward me was contained entirely within the four corners of my computer screen. After reading post after bitchy post about me and what an ugly whore I was, I expected that people might spit on me in the street or something, but that never happened.

It was sort of disappointing, actually. I wanted the opportunity to confront the people who dissed me on the Internet—to shake their hands and thank them for all the free publicity—but they never came forward to give me the satisfaction.

I ordered my skim latte at Murky Coffee "to stay." After all, I was an unemployed person with no job to go to. But what would I do now for coffee money, with no income? Would anyone pay my rent this month, or would they just let me get evicted? (If you ever get involved in a sex scandal, make sure you're financially prepared.)

I guessed I could get a job at the Gap folding jeans or something. That wouldn't be so bad, would it? I would live a simple life and make an honest living. But how long would it take for me to go absolutely insane?

I sat in the coffee shop, staring into space, wondering what to do with my life, when my phone rang.

It was Mike!

Had he heard the news? I mean, had people in *New York* heard this story? I couldn't imagine that anyone up there would even care.

I called him back right away.

"How was your birthday?" he asked.

Was this some sick joke?

"Not good," I told him.

"What happened?" he asked.

Obviously, he didn't know—which was good. That meant the story was still local. But how would I tell him? Where should I begin?

"Mike," I said, "it's really bad."

"Jackie, just tell me what it is."

"I'm involved in a sex scandal."

I didn't know how else to put it.

"*What?*" he asked. "With who, the president?"

I was flattered that Mike thought I could sleep my way to

the top like that, but the true story was pathetic in comparison. I was embarrassed to admit how low level it was.

"With some guys from work," I told him.

I realized that he didn't know that I had been working in the Senate, so I explained everything. The job, the men, the blog. Mike just listened, taking it all in. Then he spoke.

"I called you, thinking that maybe we could get back together," he told me. "I'd been thinking about you a lot lately, and I wanted to see how you were doing."

*This was a deus ex machina if there ever was one,* I thought. Mike still loved me and he wanted me back! I could catch a train back to New York right now and live happily ever after.

Then he started to laugh.

"Now I realize that I shouldn't have bothered," he said. "You're still the same screwed-up train wreck you've always been. Good luck with all of that. Just leave me out of it—don't call me, don't e-mail me, just leave me out of it."

I winced as Mike hung up on me, but I knew he was right: I really was a screwed-up train wreck—but at least I wasn't *boring.*

I realized that if Mike truly loved me, he wouldn't just throw his hands up and walk away, especially now, when I needed someone on my side.

*Chapter 31*

Three days had gone by, and I hadn't heard from Marcus. Even Fred had left messages, telling me not to be afraid of him, that he just wanted to talk. Part of me really wanted to call him back, but I couldn't let my guard down just because I was lonely.

I locked all of my doors and windows and wished that I had a stun gun, pepper spray, or at least a set of steak knives I could use for my own protection.

Suddenly, I felt like Washington was a huge Pac-Man board, and all of the guys from my blog were "ghosts" out to get me. I had to remind myself that they were probably more afraid of what I might do to them because I had the upper hand.

These DC men were smart, so they had to know that if

any of them came near me, I would have called the police *and* the press.

They were too afraid to leave detailed voice messages or send me e-mail because they knew I might use this stuff against them in some way (and I would have), so there was a communication breakdown in my favor.

And if any of them wanted to come forward and trash me in public, it would have been pointless. Everybody already knew I was a "screwed-up, lying, butt-fucking whore." *And?*

If any of them wanted to start some shit with me, I wasn't afraid to hit below the belt, and they knew it. I could only stand to gain from this, while the men had everything to lose.

Advantage: Ms. Pac-Man.

But even Ms. Pac-Man had a boyfriend, and I had no one. How could *any* man want me after what I had done?

Every time my phone rang, I hoped it was Marcus, but it was always some gossip columnist or TV news producer leaving messages in my voice mail, asking me to call them back.

How did they get my number? I assumed it had to be some other asshole who thought it would be fun to participate in my humiliation. Who knew I had so many enemies in this town?

There was one voice mail from Phillip, who sounded totally oblivious to the "sex scandal" that he was involved in— he was actually inviting me out to *dinner* that night.

I called him back, expecting him to react the same way Mike had. But Phillip was unlike any other man I had ever known.

"You know what your big mistake was?" he asked. "Not fucking some congressman!"

"Oh, *that* was my big mistake!" I laughed. "So you're not mad about this?"

"Mad? Why would I be mad? Why don't you come over to my place this afternoon, and we'll have lunch."

I wasn't sure if I should.

"Don't you want to read the blog first?" I asked. "I wrote some bad things about you. And there's all this other stuff, about me and other guys."

"Did you use my name?" he wanted to know.

I told him that I had only used initials.

"Then what's the big deal?" he asked. "It's not like I can get fired!"

True, Phillip *did* own his own law firm. But if he hadn't read the blog, how could he forgive me for something he didn't understand?

Maybe he was luring me to his house so he could murder me, I thought, but Phillip was too cool for that. And it really *wasn't* a big deal, was it? I was probably flattering myself thinking that this was something he would risk going to jail for.

I WAS SITTING ON PHILLIP'S stoop when his Mercedes pulled into the driveway.

"I read the blog," he said as he climbed out of his car.

I braced myself for a tirade of obscenities and insults.

"It's pretty funny!" he chuckled. "Especially the parts about me! Let's go inside and have ourselves a drink!"

As soon as we walked in the door, he grabbed me. At first, I was terrified, but then I realized that we were *hugging*.

"I'm sorry," he was saying. "I'm sorry, I'm so sorry."

I wasn't sure what he was apologizing for, since I was the one who had written all that mean stuff about him. I was angry with him for hurting me back in Miami, but I had never told him so. Then again, he'd read the blog.

I guess that was why he was apologizing, for hurting me.

He held on to me tightly as I shook in his arms, sobbing, getting my tears and snot all over his expensive suit.

I never thought that I would cry for *him*. All this time, I thought he was an arrogant jerk. But really, I was the arrogant one.

Once I was all cried out, I freshened myself up in the powder room and joined him for a drink in his huge stainless steel kitchen. Meanwhile, my phone kept ringing inside my handbag.

"What should I do about these calls?" I asked him. "I need your advice."

"If I were you, I would sue your office for wrongful termination," he suggested.

"Oh, Phillip, don't be such a *lawyer*. I can't sue them. They had every right to fire me, and I think any judge would agree."

"We could claim that your use of the Senate computers was common practice and subpoena everybody's computer records as evidence. We could have all of the computers in the Senate confiscated!"

It was brilliant, but somehow, it didn't seem right.

I shook my head no.

"Well, that's what *I* would do, but that's just the kind of sick bastard I am," he smiled. "It seems like you have two other choices here: You can try to cash in on whatever notoriety this thing brings you, or you can change your name and move out of Washington."

"What would you do if you were me?" I asked.

"Have some headshots taken."

"Seriously, do you really think I should come forward?" I asked to make sure I had his blessing.

"What do you have to lose? You don't want to come off like you're hiding from these reporters, now do you? You have to be brazen and shameless. People love that."

"Should I call them back?"

"Yeah, but do it later. I want to be the first to fuck Washington's newest sex scandalette."

I went upstairs with Phillip, glad to have someone on my side. It was especially validating that it was one of the men from my blog. It gave me hope: If Phillip could forgive me, then maybe the others could, too.

We had a couple more drinks as we lay around naked in his house. I called back every reporter and gave drunk interviews over the phone. When they asked me to appear on television, I said, "Sure, why not? I'm not ashamed of how I look!"

Sure, I had been drinking straight bourbon all afternoon, and I probably shouldn't have been giving interviews while under the influence, but I felt great: I was brazen and shameless, like Phillip said, and I wasn't afraid anymore. I slept like a baby that night.

·  ·  ·

"HAVE YOU HEARD FROM any of the other guys from the blog?" Phillip asked me the morning after.

"You're the only one who stuck by me," I told him.

"That's because I'm the only one who really loved you."

It was a nice thing for him to say, but I hoped it wasn't true. If only one of them truly loved me, I wanted it to be Marcus.

"So what now?" he asked. "What's your plan?"

"I don't know," I replied. "I might move to New York to get away from all this."

"*Or* you could move in with me," he offered.

"Are you serious?" I asked.

"Just think about it."

It was difficult to imagine myself living in Phillip's well-appointed townhouse. I really wasn't the "Georgetown housewife" type: I wouldn't be caught dead in a quilted Burberry jacket.

I went home, read some e-mails, made some phone calls, and set up some appointments in New York for the following week. I was going to be in town anyway: Naomi and I were going to the Fleet Week party on the *Intrepid*, like we did every year. Sex scandal or no, I just couldn't miss Fleet Week. The ships only came in once a year. Besides, I had agents in New York who wanted to make me rich. Now that I wasn't being subsidized, I could only hope my own ship would come in.

NAOMI LET ME STAY OVER at her place during this "business trip" to save me the expense of a hotel, since I was cash poor while I waited to cash in on the huge mistake that I had made. I figured I had to make the best of things, and everybody close to me agreed, especially Naomi.

"You need to make as much money off this thing as you possibly can," she advised me as we got dressed for the party. "I hope you realize how small your window is. People have very short attention spans, you know."

"They don't in DC," I said. "Everybody there is still totally obsessed with me."

"Well, DC is small-time. It's a lot harder to get famous in New York, you know. You were on 'Page Six,' like, a week ago. Do you think that anyone here still cares?"

Naomi and I tried to put together outfits with as much sailor appeal as possible. You would think that this meant anything short and tight, but after a few years of dressing for Fleet Week, Naomi and I knew what *really* made a sailor stand to attention: You had to look like that nice, sweet girl they left behind in Wichita or wherever the fuck it was they came from.

Seriously, you wore a sundress and a smile, and it worked every time. I wore one of my Lilly dresses, and Naomi wore a strapless dress that she bought at C.K. Bradley especially for this occasion.

It was a full ten degrees cooler in New York than it was in DC, so we wore cardigans over our dresses, which made us look even more adorable.

We walked in, took our sweaters off, and immediately we had company. It was too easy. Two nineteen-year-olds, fresh off the farm. Actually, I didn't know where they came from, but I always liked to think that it was from the farm. (It was part of the fantasy, you see.)

Since they didn't have ID, Naomi and I had to buy all of their drinks for them when we took them out barhopping with us. We ended up at Bourbon Street on the Upper West Side, which was always a scary place to be at four in the morning. This was when the extremely drunk, leftover single people stopped taking no for an answer. I was so tired I was about to fall asleep standing up, which was not a smart thing to do.

Christ, what was happening to me? I used to be able to stay up for three days straight, with or without drugs, and now I didn't even have the energy to make out with either of these boys?

Maybe the stress was getting to me, because I didn't even find them attractive anymore. I mean, they were just a couple of bumpkins. They weren't even my type.

"What's wrong?" Naomi asked me. "Are you about to puke?"

"No, I'm just tired," I answered. "Can I have the key to your apartment? I think I'm done here."

"Yeah, me too. Did you know they were gay?" Naomi asked, referring to the sailors. "They just wanted us to buy them drinks all night."

We had been duped by gay sailors. So not cool.

I AWOKE AROUND NOON, unrefreshed and sore. I felt like I had the flu, and I hadn't eaten in forever. I looked around Naomi's kitchen, but she was just like me: boxes of shoes in the cupboards, sweaters in the oven, nothing but booze in the fridge.

She was the one who told me that "New York girls don't eat." But I wasn't a New York girl anymore, was I?

We went to Columbia Bagel and ordered egg bagels with tofu cream cheese.

"I shouldn't even be eating this," I told Naomi. "I'm going to get fat, and then people will have yet another reason to make fun of me. I can't even leave my apartment without doing my hair and makeup anymore."

"I think you should get out of DC," Naomi said. "I mean, doesn't it suck or something?"

"But I'm moving in with Phillip."

"*What?* Why would you want to live with *that* dickhole?"

"Things are different now. At least I know he cares about me."

Naomi snorted.

"Would you listen to yourself?" she asked. "How much fun can you have living with *Phillip*? If you moved back to New York, we could go out all the time and it would be awesome. It would be just like old times!"

I thought on this. Truth was, I was no longer interested in re-creating our young-and-crazy-and-living-in-New-York phase. I was also reluctant to leave Washington. I wanted to stay in DC just to spite all those people who were trying to shame me out of town.

"But isn't living well the best revenge?" I argued. "Wouldn't it just make everybody sick to see me end up living in a mansion with some millionaire? And not just *any* millionaire, but the one from the blog who found it in his heart to forgive me. Wouldn't that be the perfect ending to all of this?"

"This isn't some *story*, Jackie. This is your *life*. Washington is not a good place for you right now. You need to get out of there. I mean, look at you!"

She held up her golden Estee Lauder compact for me to see my reflection.

"Look at your skin," she told me. "Your pores are huge. Your face looks like a damn strawberry. And look at your hair. It looks like it's about to fall out at any second. Your face even looks different—you look old. All of this stress is starting to affect your *looks*, Jackie. You're obviously not handling it as well as you think you are."

I was horrified to see that she was right. The proof was staring right back at me in the mirror.

Maybe I deserved to turn ugly. That would be the ultimate punishment for all of this. I mean, I had it coming to me, didn't I?

I always thought that everything about me was fabulous. While most people might have hypothesized that I had "degraded" myself because I had low self-esteem, the real problem was that my self-esteem was too fucking high!

Obviously, I couldn't see myself objectively, so maybe I had problems that were more than skin-deep.

# Chapter 32

I made up my mind to get professional help. When I got back to DC, I called around for a therapist, but I couldn't get an appointment for the next eight days unless I was "about to harm myself or others."

I thought about it. I sort of wanted to kill whoever it was that put my picture on the Internet, but I supposed that didn't count. I was really more the careless, self-destructive type than I was the death-fixated, suicidal type. In early eighties supermodel terms, I was more of a Gia Carangi than a Margaux Hemingway.

I agreed that my problems could wait. Give the earlier appointments to the people who truly needed them, the homicidal maniacs and the bridge-jumpers. I really wasn't that far gone yet.

But a whole new set of problems arose on my first day back in Washington.

I threw my Vera Bradley down on the floor and took a shower. I guess the bathroom noises alerted the owners of the house that I was home, because seconds later, they were banging down my front door.

Neither Fred nor Phillip had paid the last month's rent, so they were taking the matter up with me. I only had about six hundred dollars in my checking account at the time, not nearly enough to cover the two months' rent I owed, and they were furious.

"We are very unhappy with you as a tenant," one of them told me. "Your failure to pay your rent on time, on top of the fact that you were running a brothel from our basement, gives us no choice but to evict."

"But I'm not responsible for the rent!" I protested. "My name isn't on the lease!"

"Well, your guarantor isn't returning our calls," he informed me. "And if he is who we *think* he is, he's going to have a problem."

Were they threatening to expose Phillip to the press?

"I'll get him to pay you," I told them. "I'm sure that he just forgot."

"We don't want to know anything about your insane personal life," he said, "as long as you give us the money by the end of the week."

He and his wife went upstairs to their perfect Capitol Hill home, as I stood in my nearly empty, liquor-bottle-strewn apartment, wrapped in the towel I had grabbed to answer the door. *Insane personal life?*

I guess the rent was technically an oversight on my part. Legally, it was Phillip's responsibility, but it didn't matter whose name was on the lease: If nobody was cutting the checks, then *I* was the one who was going to end up out on the street.

I didn't come to Washington to end up homeless, penniless, and out of a job. I dearly hoped that Phillip had just forgotten, and that this wasn't his sick way of getting revenge on me for exposing him in my blog. But with my landlords threatening to go to the media, he would pay the rent if he knew what was good for him.

I called Phillip's office, and his secretary told me that he was away at his house in Palm Springs for the week. So I tried calling his cell phone, but he wasn't picking up. I left a totally freaked-out message on his voice mail and waited for him to call me back.

If this really was Phillip's way of screwing me over, so to speak, I couldn't let him get away with it. I had to remind him that if he wanted to keep his privacy, he would have to pay for it. He had to keep writing the checks until *I* said stop.

If only I had been an honest, hardworking, independent woman who paid her own rent, and didn't have to rely on the charity of her gentlemen callers to subsidize a lifestyle she couldn't otherwise afford.

But then I wouldn't have such nice things, so fuck that. Besides, you couldn't turn back time, now could you? Whatever bullshit you saw Ashton Kutcher pull off in *The Butterfly Effect* was not happening here.

. . .

THREE HOURS AND FOUR glasses of Wild Turkey on the rocks later, Phillip finally called me back. He told me that he had been out on the golf course all morning, where he had just finished ten under par and wasn't that just *out-standing*?

"Phillip, you forgot to pay my rent before you left for Palm Springs," I reminded him.

"Darling, I'm sorry," he chuckled. "I had a case and it totally slipped my mind. I'll take care of it when I get back."

"Um, Phillip, you're not flying back this week, are you? Because that's when my landlords want the money you owe."

"Fuck 'em—they can wait."

"Can't you just put a check in the mail or something?" I asked. "I mean, is it *that* hard?"

I imagined that this was what his ex-wife had to go through to get Phillip to pay her alimony. Just like golf, women were an expensive hobby.

"I'm on vacation right now," Phillip reminded me. "I came here to relax and get away from all that. You don't think that I'm worried about it, too? Jesus! And I have three young sons to protect."

So Phillip had *three* children. With him, you learned something new every day.

"But that's exactly why you have to send me the money today," I explained. "My landlords are threatening to name names."

At this, Phillip quickly agreed to have his secretary courier over a check. Crisis averted—until next month.

I had to get out of this place, I decided. When Phillip

came back from Palm Springs, I would move into his town-house and live happily ever after.

I WENT OUT AND BOUGHT myself a cocker spaniel puppy that afternoon. I had always wanted a dog, and since I was moving out, I could housebreak him in the apartment.

My new psychiatrist, Dr. Klein, had said that getting a pet would be "therapeutic," but I think she had an ulterior motive. I had to change my entire lifestyle when I brought that dog home. I couldn't stay out all night anymore, and I had to get up at seven o'clock every morning to take him out to pee.

Such hard work! No way I could ever have a baby—I guess I was really more of a cat person.

Dr. Klein was a tall, fine-boned woman with graying hair and bright green eyes. She wore a bright red lipstick that complemented her pale complexion, and I could tell she was the sort of woman who preferred pantsuits over skirts.

As much as I loved to talk about myself, I wanted more than just "talk therapy." I did not expect to leave her office without a prescription for happy pills in my sweaty little hand, so I came prepared: I had stopped at a Kinkos and made a copy of the *Washington Post* article featuring moi.

"This is me," I told her, putting it in front of her to read.

She adjusted the glasses on her face.

After skimming the article for a few seconds, she asked, "Why did you show this to me?"

I could tell this was one of those questions that she

already knew the answer to, but just wanted to hear my explanation so she could gain insight into my warped mind.

"I just thought that this was something that you should be aware of," I told her.

"Why don't you explain what happened to you in your own words."

I didn't even know where to begin, but as soon as I started talking, I felt the same stinging sensation I had felt when my mother told me that she had been having an affair.

"I'm sorry," I said, but I couldn't stop myself from bawling when I got to the part about Marcus.

"Obviously, this is something that is really bothering you," Dr. Klein said. "You can't even talk about it without falling apart."

"Yeah, I know," I hiccuped. "That's why I don't talk about it ever, not with my friends or anybody—it doesn't make me feel better, it just makes me feel worse!"

I grabbed a tissue and blew my nose.

"I have to ask you something," I said once I had regained some of my composure. "I need to know what's wrong with me, if I'm crazy or not."

"I can tell you right now, you're not crazy," Dr. Klein said. "You're dealing with a very upsetting situation in your life right now and—"

"I mean, before this even happened," I interrupted, "when I was sleeping around and stuff."

"You're talking about promiscuous behavior, which is not at all uncommon. Now, is that behavior something you would like to change or not?"

"I guess I just want to know if I'm normal or not."

*What a dumb question,* I thought.

"It seems like you're looking for validation for your be-havior, which isn't something that I'm able to give you," Dr. Klein told me. "What I *can* do is prescribe some pills that will help you stop giving a damn."

"Perfect!" I said excitedly.

"But I'm giving them to you on one condition: You have to start going to Alcoholics Anonymous. Jacqueline, I think you have a substance-abuse problem."

"I do?"

"If you read over your blog, I think you'll begin to see a pattern in your behavior: You've been drunk pretty much the whole time you've been here."

She was absolutely right.

"So is that what my problem is?" I asked. "I'm just an alcoholic?"

"Your problem is that you're depressed," Dr. Klein said. "And you probably have been ever since you were a child."

"Really? But why?"

"From what you've told me about your parents, it's probably hereditary."

"So I was born depressed? That's so . . . *depressing.*"

"What you have is dysthymia. It's a type of depression that's very common among people like writers and comedi-ans. People who have this disorder are constantly doing things to *entertain* themselves and others as a means to cope with their depression."

It was as if Dr. Klein had explained my whole life to me. I left her office, wishing that I had seen her sooner. Like when I was five.

.    .    .

APRIL CAME OVER WHEN she got off work that day to see the puppy, and we took him to the dog park on Fifth Street, Southeast.

"Does he have a name yet?" she asked me.

"Yeah, it's Biff," I told her. "Look, he's the worst dog in the park!"

We watched Biff as he ran up to another dog and started humping her.

"Biffy! No!" I yelled at him.

"No one wants to play with him," April observed. "Even the *dogs* in DC are boring."

"How are things at work?" I asked her. "How's Dan?"

"He's still trying to lay low. But he won't even say hello to me because he knows that I'm still friends with you. It's, like, office policy to trash you, Jackie."

I rolled my eyes.

"They're all just mad that they didn't think of it first, and they still have to go to their miserable jobs on the Hill," I said. "No offense."

I was hoping to inspire a confession from April, but all I got was an uncomfortable shrug, so I put Biff back on his leash and we walked back to my apartment.

"Have you heard anything about Marcus?" I asked. "He hasn't lost his job, has he?"

"I don't think so," April said, "but I can't imagine he'd want to stay. He's probably looking for something in the private sector, like Dan is."

"I hope so. I think it would be good for him, to get away from the Hill."

We left the dog at home and went to the Georgetown Waterfront to meet up with Laura, who had been working on a campaign down in Florida all month. April and I had to fill her in on everything she had missed.

"Well, I think you're doing the right thing," Laura told me. "Give interviews, go on TV, and have fun with it! In a way, I sort of envy you!"

"Ugh! How can you say that?" I asked her. "I envy *you*. You still have your good name."

I looked around at all the other girls on the Waterfront. Sure, they were all doing the same shit that I was—probably even worse—but they still had their innocence, and I would never have that again.

I envied all of these girls, even the fat ones.

April excused herself to take a call from Tom.

"You know that it was April, right?" Laura asked me. "She's your Linda Tripp."

"Believe me, I know," I replied.

"You do? Aren't you furious?"

"I guess I should be, but I know that this is eating her up inside. She feels bad enough."

"You think so?"

"Yeah, it's pretty obvious. She keeps paying for all my drinks."

Drunk guys stopped by our table and asked to have their pictures taken with me or whatever, but they didn't hit on me as much as they used to. It was somewhat dispiriting to realize that my bad reputation was a turnoff for the majority of guys in Washington.

"What is wrong with the men in DC?" Laura wondered.

"I thought that you would get tons of dates as a result of this."

"Yeah, I'll need to move back to New York if I ever want to hook up with a stranger again," I pouted.

April returned to the table, insisting that we go to the Tiki Bar at Third Edition, where she was meeting Tom.

Not an hour after we arrived, a very pretty blond South African boy invited me back to his hotel room. He was in town for a wedding, still wearing the tuxedo he had worn for the ceremony. Some South African diplomat's daughter had married the son of an attaché or something—anyway, it sounded lovely, and they were all staying at the Mayflower.

"Are you hungry?" he asked in his funny South African accent. "I am famished."

I wasn't eating anything, but I stood in line with him at Julia's Empanadas on Connecticut Avenue.

"Are you Jacqueline Turner?" asked the guy waiting behind us.

I didn't recognize him from anywhere, but I nodded yes.

Then I remembered, I was *that* Jacqueline Turner, the one with the sex blog: I didn't know him, but he knew me.

"You are? Cool!" the guy said, handing me his business card. "Call me. We should hang out."

The South African looked confused.

"How does he know you?" he asked.

I imagined that I would have a lot of explaining to do from now on, but this was my first time explaining it to a potential love interest. I half-expected him to freak out, but he still just looked confused.

"I don't get it," he said. "Why is this a big deal? Who gives a shit?"

"*Exactly,*" I told him. "I don't get it either."

"Fucking Americans," he scoffed.

I went back to his hotel room, where we got under the sheets and cracked jokes in bed for a while. He was a lot of fun, and I wished that he wasn't going back to Johannesburg the next day.

Eventually, we stopped joking around, and he climbed on top of me. We had taken our clothes off about half an hour prior, so we had built up a lot of anticipation, taking peeks and brushing up against each other in the bed.

"Do you have condoms?" I asked.

"No, I don't," he said. "Don't you?"

I sighed and shook my head no.

"But Americans always have condoms," he said.

"Do we?" I asked.

Then why didn't any of the guys I knew ever seem to have any?

We had a frustratingly chaste makeout session until my cell phone went off. It was Laura, who was calling me from the George Washington University Hospital.

## Chapter 33

I spent the night in the waiting room, scoping out cute doctors with Laura until the nurses let us into detox, where they were keeping April.

Tom marched out of the room with a scowl on his face.

"How is she?" I asked him, but he blew right by me on his way toward the exit.

The nurse said that April was asking for me, so I got up from the chair that I was curled up in and went in to see her.

She was lying on a cot with an IV of fluids hooked up to her arm. Her face was red and puffy, and I could tell that she had been crying.

"Tom just dumped me!" she sobbed.

"He dumped you *here*?" I asked.

April nodded.

"He said that he could never marry someone like me because he wants to run for Congress someday!" she said. "He says that I'm an embarrassment!"

It was the most disgusting thing I had ever heard. If Tom had cared about anyone besides himself, he would have tried to *help* April, not throw her away like some used jizz rag.

"I'm a mess!" she wailed when she saw the huge purple bruises on her arms from the IV.

"That's just, like, his opinion, April. This happens to everyone," I said, trying to comfort her. "I've woken up in the hospital plenty of times—it's no biggie."

"Oh, shut up!" she said. "It's a big deal to me! What kind of a friend are you anyway?"

"What kind of a friend am *I*?" I asked. "How dare you even ask that question! You, of all people!"

"What are you talking about?"

"April, I *know* it was you."

"Huh?"

"You were the one who outed my blog. You ruined my life, you realize."

"What are you talking about?" she asked. "Your life isn't *ruined*. You're much better off than you were before."

I probably *was* better off than I was back in May, sorting mail for some senator who I secretly thought was an asshole, fucking guys who I secretly thought were assholes, too. But if I was better off, why was I still so angry? At that moment, I wanted to rip her arm off and beat her to death with it, Prozac or no.

"It wasn't your choice to make!" I finally said. "You had no right to do what you did!"

"I feel bad enough already," April broke down. "Can't you let it go?"

"Well, you should feel bad," I said.

"Get out," April said, turning her back to me as she rolled over in her cot. "Maybe I'll call you tomorrow. Maybe not. I'm not sure I want to be friends with you anymore."


SORE FROM SLEEPING ON the waiting room chairs, I fell into bed when I got back to my apartment. Biff was crying, trying to climb up into the bed with me. I reached over to pull him up, but I dropped him on the floor: He smelled awful.

Biff had pissed all over the kitchen floor because I hadn't come home last night to take him out. My apartment smelled like a kennel, and his food and water dishes were empty. I felt like the most incompetent person in the world. I was totally incapable of caring for anyone beside myself.

I fell asleep as my puppy cried for attention.

So much for having a friend in Washington.

I jumped out of bed when my phone rang five minutes later.

"Can you explain why there's a camera crew on my front lawn?"

It was my father, and he sounded pissed.

I hadn't told him about the blog or anything. I didn't think it had anything to do with my parents, but apparently, the local news media thought differently: They wanted to know how my father felt about his little girl having lewd sex in exchange for money in DC.

When I started to explain, he stopped me, much to my relief.

"When did you intend to tell me this?" he asked.

"I didn't think I—"

"That's right," he said, "you *didn't* think."

I suddenly felt guilty about my "brazen and shameless" act. It seemed like a good media strategy, but I never stopped to think about how my parents might feel about it, because that's not what brazen and shameless girls do.

"You're my daughter, Jackie, but you're not my little girl anymore," he told me. "I don't know what happened to you, but you're not the young woman that *I* raised. I think you should spend the holidays with your mother from now on."

Spending the holidays with my mother was like going over to the Dark Side: I didn't want to be like *her*, but that's what my father saw when he saw my picture in the newspapers: a girl who was just like her lying, cheating mother.

I SPENT THE NEXT FEW days holed up in my bedroom, crying into my pillow, with "Against All Odds" by Phil Collins playing on repeat in my CD player. It was pathetic.

I didn't even know what I was crying about most of the time, but I was miserable.

Janet was right about me: I really was a piece of shit. I pretended that I was some sort of glamour girl when I went on TV and posed for photographers, but the truth was not so pretty.

"The Washingtonienne" was a girl who knew that pussy was power—a walking Id with a huge Ego. She was me, but she wasn't me. I had stopped being that girl when I started dating Marcus.

When I was with Marcus, I felt like I could be myself. But if I was lying and cheating the whole time, what did that even mean?

*That* was why I could not stop crying: I didn't know *who* I was anymore. I felt like the biggest phony in Washington. How did all these politicians do it?

April finally called me, on the third day of my Phil Collins marathon.

"I owe you an apology," she said. "I'm sorry I—"

"No, I owe *you* an apology," I interrupted her. "You were in the hospital, Tom just dumped you, and all I could think about was myself."

"But you were right! I shouldn't have done that to you. God, I feel like such a bad person."

"April, you are *not* a bad person! There's no such thing as a 'bad person' anyway. I mean, no one is *that* consistent in their behavior. We just fucked shit up—big-time."

"You have to know that I didn't mean for any of this to happen. I thought that everyone would think your blog was funny— I didn't know that people would be such bitches about it."

"Well, people are stupid—how totally shocking."

"Yeah, I should have known better. I mean, I work on the Hill *and* I talk to idiots on the phone all day!"

I started to laugh, and now we were two crazy girls, giggling about all the trouble that we had caused.

"So you and Tom are finished?" I asked.

"Yeah," April sighed. "I'm quitting the office, too. Dan is acting like a total prick toward me, and Tom is trying to get me fired. He told the chief of staff that I was on drugs! Luckily, my dealer works on the Hill, too, so there were no suspicious numbers in my phone records because they were all interoffice calls.

"But he was right: I *do* have a problem. I should probably go to AA or something."

"That's what my therapist says! Will you come with me tonight?" I begged. "I really need to get out of my apartment."

"Do you even know what they make you do there?" April asked. "You have to tell everyone stories about all the fucked-up stuff you did while you were drunk."

At this, I laughed.

"That's easy! I'll just pass out copies of all those newspaper articles about me."

"And you know what else?" April asked. "You have to make amends with all the people who you've wronged while you were drunk."

I had forgotten all about Step Nine of the Twelve Steps of Alcoholics Anonymous. I imagined calling up Mike, Dan, the senator. And Marcus.

"I probably shouldn't go," I said.

"But don't you want to see who else is there?" April asked. "Even if we hate it, at least we'll find out who else in this town has hit rock bottom."

I had to admit, I was curious.


AS WE CLIMBED THE STAIRS to the meeting space above the gay bookstore in Dupont Circle, I reminded April that we couldn't go out for drinks after the meeting.

"We'll just have to sit somewhere and eat something," I told her.

"AA is going to make us fat," she surmised.

"Maybe we should just go home afterward," I said as we walked into a room filled with folding chairs.

Then I saw something that made me turn around and go home early.

Sitting across the room was Marcus.

And he knew that I was running away because April was yelling after me, *"Jackie, where are you going?"*

I didn't know that Marcus was in Alcoholics Anonymous, and I guess that's the point. I mean, I knew that he didn't drink, he just never told me that he was in *recovery*.

He caught me at the bottom of the stairs, grabbing my arm from behind. I knew I would cry if he started yelling, so I gathered up my courage and turned to face him.

"Is there something you want to say to me?" I asked defensively.

"No," he said, "I just wanted to see you."

I had known Marcus would never be able to look at me the same way after what had happened. And now that we were here, standing face-to-face again, he *did* look at me differently, as if he was seeing the real me for the first time.

"Please don't look at me," I winced, turning away from him. He didn't stop me this time, so I pushed the door open and started down the street toward the Metro station.

Marcus was just a few steps behind.

He was following me. Didn't that mean something? I had to turn around. But what could I say?

"You don't need to apologize," he said, reading my mind. "Do you want to talk?"

"I do, but I don't know," I replied. "I don't want to get you in any more trouble."

"Yeah, Janet would shit if she knew I was talking to you right now," he admitted.

"You're still in the office?" I asked. "How is it over there?"

"It's pretty chaotic, with you on TV and everything."

"You saw me?"

"Yeah, you looked good."

I was amazed that he could still find me attractive—this meant something, too. Maybe I really *could* win him back. He had been so understanding about the spanking rumor before, maybe he could get over this, too. And if Phillip could forgive me, it was not impossible that Marcus could do the same.

His forgiveness would be the ultimate validation. I realized that it was probably wrong to entertain these ideas, but when I was with him, I couldn't help it: I always wanted what I couldn't have, and Marcus was the most unattainable man in the world to me right now.

"So why haven't you called?" I wanted to know.

"I was waiting for you to call me," he replied, "but as the days went by, and I didn't hear from you, I assumed that you didn't care."

"Of course I care! I was just afraid."

"Then why did you go on television and laugh about it?" he asked. "You didn't look scared to me! And if you really cared, you wouldn't have done that—you wouldn't have done any of this!"

We were having this argument in the middle of Dupont Circle, and I was afraid we might make a spectacle out of ourselves.

"Can we talk about this at my place?" I asked.

We ended up having the best sex of our lives.

*Chapter 34*

The next morning, we made plans to move to New York, where we could both start over. Marcus would get a job at a law firm, and I would . . . do what exactly, I didn't know.

"This is our chance for a fresh start," he told me. "I don't want you pursuing any book or movie deals, or doing anything related to the blog. I just want to forget this ever happened."

"Then what am I supposed to do with my life?" I asked. "I can't get a job anywhere, I'm a laughingstock! Why shouldn't I make money off this mess?"

He went on to tell me about some episode of *True Life* he had seen on MTV, about a crack-addicted porn star who had turned her life around by leaving the skin-flick industry, going back to school, and becoming a counselor for teen prostitutes or whatever.

I did not appreciate the analogy he was making.

"All I'm saying is that you have other options," he said.

Since I was willing to do anything to win Marcus back, I agreed to go back to school. I wasn't one to turn away from love, even when I knew it might not work out.

My friends were furious when I informed them of my decision not to pursue the media deals that were being thrown my way.

"You went through all of that bullshit, just to end up with *Marcus*?" Diane asked incredulously.

"Why is that so hard to believe?" I wanted to know.

"It just seems like you're not thinking clearly. Have you been taking your medication?"

"*Yes*," I replied firmly. "I'm not crazy, you know."

"Jackie, you're the craziest person I know—that's why Naomi and I are friends with you! But you're just not yourself right now."

"What does that even mean?" I asked. "This is me, being myself, and this is what I want to do."

"Jackie, I will not let you pass up a once-in-a-lifetime opportunity! Honestly, I cannot believe that you would even consider it!"

"But I love him, Di."

"I don't want to see you end up heartbroken," Diane warned me. "You'll end up with nothing but regrets. Before you do anything, I think you should talk this over with your doctor."

I called up April and Naomi, who said pretty much the

same thing as Diane. I thought they would all be happy for me, but instead, they scolded me for taking my eyes off the prize: the chance to use my newfound fame to become independently wealthy.

"If Marcus loved you, he would let you do it. You never know, he could be playing you," Naomi warned.

"But when we were in bed last night," I sighed. "You can't fake that."

"Are you serious?" Naomi chortled. "How many orgasms have you faked in your life? Jesus, don't be so naïve."

I went to Dr. Klein's office later that day, sobbing about how confused I was.

"I don't want to make the wrong decision!" I cried. "What should I do?"

"I can't tell you what to do," she replied, "but I can tell that you have mixed feelings about going to New York with Marcus."

"It's my friends—they have me all mixed up!"

"Forget about your friends for now. Forget Marcus, too. You have to be true to yourself, Jackie."

I nodded, but it was obvious to Dr. Klein that I was a basket case. I couldn't trust my own instincts anymore because they had led me to disaster.

"Why is it so important for you to be with Marcus? It isn't as if he were the last man on Earth," she reminded me. "Nevertheless, you seem terrified of losing him. Can you tell me what makes him exceptional?"

"I can't exactly *quantify* it," I replied, "it's just—he's *different*."

"How is he different from other men you've known?"

I shrugged.

"He's nice," was all I could come up with.

"And the other men weren't nice to you?" Dr. Klein asked.

"No, not really," I replied. "Most of them were total douchebags."

"Maybe that's because you weren't very nice to them," Dr. Klein surmised. "I think what's missing here is *respect*. You seem to have a profound disrespect for men."

"You mean, I'm a *man-hater*?" I asked.

"I think that you objectify men."

"Not to trivialize this," I said defensively, "but aren't people objectifying each other all the time?"

"Is that your perception?"

"Of course it is! You're a woman, Dr. Klein. Don't you feel it?"

"But how does that make *you* feel, Jacqueline?"

"I hate it," I replied. "I hate that women are stuck on this planet with such awful creatures as men."

"So do you think that it's fair to treat men with the same disrespect? Do you think that it's right?"

I shrugged.

"I think I'm just running around in circles," I admitted.

I grabbed a tissue and waited for Dr. Klein's response. She sighed and shook her head at me.

"Then why don't you just stop?" she asked. "Take a break from men. If they're such 'awful creatures,' why not eliminate them from your life altogether?"

"But I can't give up on men," I told her. "I want love."

I hated to admit it, but it was the truth: I knew only

stupid girls fell in love with the men they slept with, but I had somehow managed to make that mistake.

I left Dr. Klein's office with a prescription for Zoloft and a grudge against Marcus for making me choose between love and money: There was no reason I couldn't have both.

I WENT BACK TO MY apartment and pouted for about an hour before there was a knock on my door.

I tiptoed over to the living room window to see who it was.

"Jacqueline?"

*Fuck!*

He saw me.

Fred was at my door, reaching into his pocket for the key.

"Jacqueline, I have to talk to you!"

"Go away!" I shrieked. "I don't want to talk to you! If you come in here, I'm calling the cops!"

I scrambled toward my bedroom, where my cell phone was on the nightstand, but Fred was already inside the apartment.

I kicked and scratched at him when he grabbed me, terrified that he had come here to strangle me, or slash my face with a razor blade. (Which is what *I* would have done if I were him!)

He put his hand over my mouth, and I thought, *This is it. This is how it's going to end. Well, I'm ready. Bring it on.*

I stopped struggling and looked Fred in the eye. What was he waiting for? *Do it.*

"Jacqueline, I'm not going to hurt you," he said, keeping his hand over my mouth. "Just listen to me."

He let go of me and we sat on my living room floor. (I still didn't have any furniture.) It was the first time I had ever seen him in his "casual clothes." He actually looked sort of cool, sitting there, playing with my puppy, who had turned out to be an ineffective guard dog.

"We need to talk," he said.

"Why aren't you at work?" I asked him. "Did anyone find out about this?"

"It hasn't even come up there, but my wife knows. She saw your picture in the *Post* and remembered that I had your number in my BlackBerry."

I had forgotten all about that. I might not have come forward if I had remembered. But at the time, I could only worry about myself.

"Jesus, Fred. I'm sorry," I told him. "But you have to know that I never meant for this to happen."

"So you didn't plan this?" he asked.

"You think I *wanted* any of this to happen?"

"No," he replied. "I know you better than that. But Jill wants a divorce. She'll probably get everything."

"Jill is your wife?"

He nodded. I had never heard him say her name before.

"So what are you going to do?" I asked him. "Are you staying in Washington?"

"I want to get out of here, but I'm waiting to hand in my resignation. It wouldn't be prudent to act now, but if we lose the election this year, I'll lose my job anyway. What about you? Are you leaving?"

I shrugged.

"I really don't know what I'm going to do," I told him.

"Why don't you move to New York with me?" Fred asked. "We could get a place in your name and just *disappear*."

I could not believe that he was serious.

"What about your baby?" I asked. "You're never going to see him again?"

"It's a *her*, actually. But she doesn't need someone like me in her life."

Why was I more concerned about Fred's family than he was? Fred disgusted me, but even more so, I was disgusted with myself for putting myself in this situation.

"Fred, we can't do this," I told him.

"You *owe* me," he said. "After what you did to me and my family—"

"What *I* did? You did this to yourself!"

Fred got up from the floor and stood over me.

"You didn't keep up your end of the deal," he said.

"So what? You're going to kill me if I don't give you your money back?"

Fred looked down at me and scowled.

"You're not worth it," he said, and he kicked my dog on his way out.

"I can't believe the president would be friends with someone like you!" I shouted after him, and he slammed the door hard enough to make the room shake.


I PUT BIFF IN HIS Kate Spade carrier, grabbed my bikini, and caught a cab to the Omni-Shoreham in Woodley Park, the hotel with the nicest pool in town. (On hot days, the girls and I would talk stray male guests into signing us in.) From the patio, I called up Laura and asked if I could stay at her place for the next few nights.

"You should report Fred to the police," Laura said, "or send his name to Blogette!"

"I don't want to piss him off! Now he has nothing to lose and I'm afraid he'll come back," I told her.

"You can stay over, but I don't have much room since April moved in. She got evicted from her apartment last week because she couldn't make the rent."

"Why didn't she tell me?" I asked.

"She didn't want to ask you for any favors because she still feels guilty. But don't worry about April—I got her a job at my firm," Laura told me. "*You're* the one I worry about."

"You do?" I asked, surprised that Laura even cared.

"Of course, Jackie! You're the closest female friend I have. We've been through some pretty crazy shit together—I mean, we've seen each other *naked*!"

I realized just how much we were alike, we Capitol Hill career girls who came from meager beginnings, with nothing but our feminine wiles to help us get ahead in this town. Players knew game when they saw it, which made us competitors first, friends second.

Laura and I never got past the sexual politics that prevented us from having a true friendship, which was something I always regretted: Women could forgive men for almost any terrible thing that they did to us, but when it came to each other, we just weren't worth the effort.

I told Laura that I would ask Marcus if I could stay at his place instead, and she said, "I just know things will work out with him—I could tell, he would do anything to make you happy."

She wished me luck, as if she knew that we would never speak again. But whatever, bygones were bygones.

So I called Marcus at work and told him about what happened with Fred.

"Are you okay? Where are you right now?" he asked.

"I'm at the pool," I told him. "Can anyone in the office overhear you talking to me?"

"No, I'm here alone."

"Are you okay?" I asked.

He sounded strange to me.

"I got a prank phone call from some radio station this morning," he told me.

"Was it on the air?"

"I would assume so."

"That's awful. What did they say?"

"I don't remember. They said something about the blog and then I hung up."

"You hung up on them? That was probably the *worst* thing you could have done."

"What was I supposed to do? Have a conversation with them on live radio while I was at work? Now I can't even answer my phone."

"I'm sorry, Marcus. I wish there was something I could do. It's beyond my control."

"I just want it to stop," he said, "but I think you want it to keep going."

"No, I don't!" I protested. "I hate this."

"Then why do you keep feeding into it? You give all

these interviews, attracting all this attention to yourself and the blog—it's like you *want* people to read it!"

Marcus was right. My attitude up until this point was, "Why *not* feed into it?" I didn't care if people knew my shit anymore, but I realized that it wasn't just *my* shit that people were interested in. Degrading myself was one thing—if a woman did it to herself, she was in control. But I was humiliating a bunch of other people along with me, in effect, *victimizing* them.

I didn't give a damn about the senator and his office, and I guess I never really did in the first place. But I still cared about Marcus. If he wanted me to stop shooting my mouth off to every reporter who called, I owed him at least that much.

"You know, my friends are upset that we're talking," he told me. "They know that I still have feelings for you."

"Did you tell anybody about last night?" I asked.

"I'm not sure if I want anyone to know."

"Marcus, this is hard for me to hear," I told him. "Do you think you can ever forgive me?"

"Jackie, I'm still on your side, in spite of everything you do."

I wanted to believe this was true. I wanted to believe it so badly.

WE SPENT THE NIGHT together, the two of us going over the blog line by line. It was one of the hardest things I ever had to do—he was a lawyer, after all. He questioned me for hours about everything I had written—who the other guys were, what the nature of those relationships were, et cetera.

I was exhausted by the time we worked backward to my first entry, but in the end, all we could do was laugh about it.

"I can't believe you called Janet a 'pimp.' She was really pissed about that," Marcus told me.

"Why didn't you just ask me out yourself?" I wanted to know.

"I didn't know that she was going to do that!"

"Then why did she?"

I wondered what the hell was going on here.

"When you first came to the office, Janet called me up and said, 'Marcus, you have to see the new girl.'"

"*What?*" I balked. "People do that?"

"So I went over to the mailroom to check you out," Marcus continued. "I thought you were attractive, but I sort of put it out of my mind because I wasn't sure if I should date someone from the office."

"Oh, my God," I said.

I felt awful.

"Then I saw you in the conference room that day, and I said to Janet, 'That Jacqueline is pretty hot.' Then she took it upon herself to ask you out for drinks. It wasn't my idea."

"So you didn't even want to go out with me?" I asked him.

"I probably never would have asked you out."

I couldn't help but be crestfallen to hear this.

"But every day, I was liking what I saw more and more. But when I saw *this*," he said, holding up the hard copy of my blog, "I felt as if I didn't know you at all."

"And I don't know you, either," I said, "which is why I can't go to the City with you."

"You're staying in Washington?"

"I mean, I'm going to New York—just not with you."

Marcus stood up, grabbed a pillow from the bed, and went downstairs to sleep on the couch. He left for work the next morning without saying a word to me, and I woke up alone in his empty house, wondering if I had made another huge mistake.

I WAS STILL AFRAID TO go back to my apartment, with Fred still at large. My rent was due and I didn't really feel like paying it, so I called Phillip to ask what he wanted to do about it.

"I knew you'd leave me stuck with that place," he complained. "Usually, it's the transients who get ripped off when they come to DC, not the other way around!"

"I'm sorry, Phillip, but I just can't stay there anymore. Can you come with me to get my things, and I'll stay with you until I go to New York on Thursday."

"This isn't a good week for me," he said. "I have the kids here, and Penelope would go ballistic if she found out you were staying in the house with them."

"But I thought you wanted me to move in with you."

"Yeah, I was just being selfish, wanting you to stay here. But both you and I know that you're too young for me. You'd end up breaking my heart."

"So what should I do?"

"You should call that guy from your office who you were so in love with—the one from your blog."

"So you don't want me anymore?" I asked. "I thought you said you loved me."

"I loved you just as much as you loved me," he replied. "I'm not going to make you happy, Jackie. You're looking for true love, and I gave up on that concept a long time ago. I'm a selfish bastard, and I'll only make you miserable. Go find yourself a nice guy, and if it doesn't work out, well, you always have my card."

I knew that Phillip was trying to do the right thing, but I still felt dissed: He was abandoning me *because* he cared about me, only he cared about himself more. Obviously, he was afraid of getting ripped off again.

I was getting desperate here. When I went back to Dr. Klein's office, I told her that I couldn't afford to continue treatment.

"Have you asked your parents for financial help?" she asked. "You look like you haven't been eating."

"Oh, I *always* look like this," I boasted. "But, no, I can't ask my parents for help. We're estranged right now."

"Are they upset about the blog? Some parents have difficulty dealing with the fact that their children have a sexual life."

"It's *not* that—my parents are totally cool. It's just my mother—she cheated on my father."

Then I lost it: Tears and mucus spewed from my face, and my makeup was ruined.

"I don't know why I'm crying!" I sobbed. "I mean, this is nothing—people cheat all the time!"

"Obviously, it's *something*, or else you wouldn't be falling apart right now," Dr. Klein replied.

"I'm crazy, aren't I? There's something very wrong with me!"

"Why is it easier for you to believe that you're crazy than it is for you to admit you've done something wrong?"

"Me? But I didn't—"

I had to stop myself. I realized that I *did* do something wrong.

It may have seemed pretty basic (lying + cheating = bad), but life experience had taught me otherwise. The lesson I learned was: *You can get whatever you want for free by lying and cheating, and there are never any consequences.*

When Mike broke off our engagement, the way out of my dire situation was by lying and cheating—and it worked! Now I was a *celebrated* liar/cheater who had fooled everyone, and it was their own stupid fault for being duped so easily by a pretty face.

But was my father a dupe for loving my mother? No, but my mother had the will to cause him pain anyway. It was a gross abuse of power in an unkind, unjust world.

But that's the world we live in, and that's what we all have to work with.

MY MOTHER CAME TO Washington to help me pack up my apartment. It was the first time any of my family had come to visit me since I had moved here. I guess they assumed that I could take care of myself. I was my mother's daughter, after all.

"Your father should be helping you with this," she complained as we heaved my wardrobe boxes out of my apartment.

"He's still mad," I told her. "I tried calling him first, before I talked to you, but he didn't take the call."

"He's your father—the only man a girl can ever count on

in her life. He'll get over it. The people who love you will always love you, no matter what."

We packed as much of my stuff that could fit into the back of her BMW SUV as possible, and I watched her drive away with my dog in the passenger seat.

I knew what I had to do.

I didn't change clothes or do my hair, because if he loved me, he would always love me, no matter what. I walked over to the Senate office buildings in my denim capris and Patricia Field T-shirt and lined up behind the clean-cut boys and girls who still worked here.

My flip-flops slapped across the marble floor as I padded toward the Russell Building. On the way back to Marcus's office, the kids stared and whispered, but I didn't pay attention to them. I was on a mission to get my man back.

If you ever visit the congressional office buildings, you might be interested to know that most of those solemn-looking wooden doors are unlocked, so if you ever want to surprise some pampered paper-pushers, feel free to try the knobs.

When I opened the door to Marcus's office, no one even looked up. Everyone was busy looking at stuff on the Internet. Marcus was leaning back in his chair, stretching, with Blogette on his computer screen.

"Marcus?" I said, and he jumped in his chair.

Everybody in the room stopped and stared, unsure of what to do, as Marcus rushed me out into the hallway.

"Are you crazy?" he asked. "What are you doing here?"

We went into the empty conference room where I felt as if I were lobbying Marcus to take me back.

"I'm going to New York," I told him. "Like, right now."

"Well, I can't run away with you if that's what you came here to ask me," he said. "I have work to do."

"What is it that you do exactly? I've always wondered."

"When we're not answering phone calls from disc jockeys and gossip columnists, we find time to write legislation here, Jackie."

"Really? Wow, that sounds important."

"It *is* important, and now I can't get anything done because of the scandal."

"I'm sorry about the phone calls, but it's beyond my control."

"The latest rumor is that you and your friends planned this whole thing. Is it true?"

"It was beyond my control," was all I could say, like that John Malkovich character from *Dangerous Liaisons.*

"Jackie, I have to resign. Things are very uncomfortable for me here. I'm moving back to New York once my house is sold."

"Oh, my God, I've ruined your life."

"Just do the right thing. Don't keep pursuing this."

*"The right thing?"* I repeated. "Is it right to let a bunch of blog nerds ruin my life, too? I don't think so."

"I'm not trying to tell you what to do, Jackie. Obviously, we have a conflict of interest here. I have my agenda, and you have yours. Only, I'm not sure what yours is exactly. What are you still doing here? Shouldn't you be lying on a beach somewhere?"

"I want to win you back," I told him, "but now I see that it's pointless because you're still mad at me."

"Well, quit jerking me around! Do you want to do this or not?"

"Yes, but we have to do it my way."

"I thought we agreed to forget about all of this blog business. Were you lying then, or are you lying now?"

"We could make lots of money," I argued, "and if we don't take this opportunity now, I'm afraid of what may happen to us later."

"Why are you fighting me on this? I want to be with you, and you're making it so hard."

"Well, this is me," I told him. "Can you live with it or not?"

"No, I don't think I can. I need to walk away from you, and you need to walk away from me."

He didn't even need to think about it.

"Well, it's your loss," I told him.

I wrote Naomi's address on a Post-it and stuck it on the conference room door.

"This is where I'm living until I find my own apartment," I explained. "When you move back to the City, stop by if you're ever in Morningside Heights."

"You mean *Harlem*," he said, reading the address.

"Whatever. Don't be a stranger."

We parted ways in those marble corridors that were "the perfect place to meet boys and show off my outfits," according to what I had written in my blog. Of course, I was a very different girl then, but despite everything that happened to me, I already felt nostalgia for this place. For a very brief time, I had been happy here, probably the happiest I had ever been in my whole life. And now I was walking away from the one person who still meant something to me, and he was letting me.


I HAD MISSED MY RIDE back to the City with my mother, so I walked down to Union Station to catch the Acela. Unfortunately, the station was being evacuated for a bomb threat just as I arrived. So I called April to see if she wanted to get a coffee or something, but then I remembered that she didn't work on the Hill anymore.

It occurred to me that I had no more friends left here, just enemies. This place was finished for me—for a few years anyway. Two years, four years, six years: There would always be fresh meat coming into our nation's capital in the meantime. Ours was a government of laws, not men, after all.

So I was prepared to leave Washington the same way I came: alone, heartbroken, but determined to get the most out of life while I still had time.

Sitting outside of Union Station, admiring the perfectly manicured grounds surrounding me, it was hard not to notice that the landscape was strewn with dozens of homeless people.

"There's so many of them!" all the tourists would marvel as they stepped off their tour buses in front of the station.

I guess everyone thought Washington was supposed to be perfect because *America* was supposed to be perfect, but who were we trying to kid? That was the problem with having too much pride: In the end, you're only duping yourself.

I never wanted to fall in love. Only stupid girls compromised themselves that way, and I was too smart to sell myself short.

But then again, I never could resist the urge that I was missing out on something. If there really was something to this love thing, I was going to find out about it.

*I'll get him back*, I thought. *I don't know how, but I will.*

Because as much as I hated those desperate women who chased after love, I finally had to admit that I was one of them.

But then, that's just between us girls.

# Acknowledgments

Thanks to my editor, Kelly Notaras, and my agents Michael Carlisle and Pilar Queen of Inkwell Management. I was very lucky to have you on my side, along with the team at Hyperion. Thank you all for your faith and patience.

My love to my family and friends, especially Michelle and Rachel, and special thanks to Richard Leiby at the *Washington Post*. (I'm not mad anymore.)

Last but not least, thanks to all of the bloggers who gave me so much attention and free publicity, and to all of my colleagues in Washington who sent in tips. I knew that all I had to do was wait, and you would make all of this possible.